Readers are requested to take great care of the item while in their possession, and to point out any defects that they may notice in them to the librarian.

This item should be returned on or before the latest date stamped below, but an extension of the period of loan may be granted when desired.

Date of return	Date of return	Date of return
5 OCT 2013		
2 6 OCT 2013		
1 0 JUN 2022		

Also by Berlie Doherty and published by Catnip:

Granny was a Buffer Girl
The Sailing Ship Tree
Children of Winter

For younger readers:

Peak Dale Farm: A Calf called Valentine
Peak Dale Farm: Valentine's Day

Jeannie of
White Peak Farm

Berlie Doherty

CATNIP BOOKS
Published by Catnip Publishing Ltd.
14 Greville Street
London EC1N 8SB

This edition published 2009
1 3 5 7 9 10 8 6 4 2

A CIP catalogue record for this book is available from the British Library

ISBN 978-1-846470-81-3

Printed in Poland

www.catnippublishing.co.uk

For Gerry

Contents

With thanks to David Sheasby,
who asked me to write *White Peak
Farm* for BBC Radio Sheffield;
to Gillian Hush, who broadcast
'Gran' and 'The Time Field' on
Radio 4's Morning Story; to Jane
Nissen, my editor; and to the
students of Hope Valley College
in Derbyshire, who talked to me
about their farms.

Gran

My home is on a farm in the soft folding hills of Derbyshire. Not far from us the dark peaks of the Pennines rise up into the ridge that is called the spine of England. We've always lived there; my father's family has owned the farm for generations. He never wants to let it go.

Nothing ever seemed to change there. The seasons printed their patterns on the fields, the sky cast its different lights across the moors, but our lives, I thought, would never change. Mum, Dad, Kathleen, Martin, Marion and I; Aunt Jessie and Gran. And yet, about four years ago that change did come to us, casting its different lights across the pattern of our lives. I suppose it all started with Gran.

* * *

My gran lived behind the church, in the cottage where my mother and all her sisters had been born. My gran was a gentle soul who'd once had wild and wilful ways and who had made my mother the way she is, a cut above the rest, my father says. When my gran was a girl she went to Oxford University, and was the pride of the village and the honour of her family; but hardly a year later she came back because her mother had been taken ill, and she had to nurse her through her long last illness. She stored her university books away in a chest and never spoke of them again. She took a job helping in the village school, and married the lad who had always lived next door to her. After he had given her five daughters he went away to France and was killed in the war, and she never spoke of him again either.

One day when I was at her cottage a Welsh gypsy came to the door and told her she should have been a writing lady, and Gran laughed and said that information was worth two yards of lace, provided there was no nylon in it; but when she came back in, her voice was scarcely steady enough to tell me that I must never listen to a Welsh gypsy, 'They trap the particles of your soul'.

But Gran often spoke as if she knew more than she had a right to know. When I was fourteen she told me that in ten years' time I would be a beautiful woman. That was two years ago and so far there's no indication that her opinion was based on any evidence; but for all that my secret lurks behind the mirror on the dressing-table, and smiles at me when my sisters are asleep.

And when Kathleen was courting her first boyfriend and brimming with joy about it all, Gran told me she was 'cultivating for herself an inevitable sadness', and sure enough, I found out that in the darkness of the night, Kathleen cries.

Gran left us last summer, and she announced her intentions of going one Sunday in late March, when she and my mother and I were picking wild daffodils to bring into the house for Marion's party.

'I'm going to sell my house,' she told us. 'How much d'you think I should ask for it?'

My mother was cautious, thinking at first that Gran's intentions were to move in with us, and not wishing to hurt her feelings.

'Is that wise, Mother?' she said. 'You've so much furniture . . .'

'Oh, I'll sell that stuff with the house. I've no need of that, not where I'm going.'

Gran stalked back through the long grass to the house, and the matter was not raised again until teatime, and my father back home, when she asked him the same question.

'John, I'm selling my house. How much is it worth?'

'What do you want to sell your house for? At your age?'

'Because I need the money . . .'

'If you're short, Mother, you've only to ask . . .'

She threatened to go back home without finishing the birthday tea because no one would answer a civil question seriously, and she supposed she would have to consult a solicitor, even though she suspected they were all rogues.

My mother told her that we couldn't answer her question because we had no idea, and that was the truth, but that we had a right to know why she was wanting to sell her house anyway, and where, she added carefully, she was thinking of going when she had sold it.

'I've made plans,' she said. 'I've held them in my head for over fifty years. I'm not going to change my mind now.'

My father said that if she was going to get all enigmatic about it he'd rather get off to the lambing shed, where he'd left my brother in charge of a sick ewe, but she stayed him with her next remark.

'My intentions are to go travelling.'

'Travelling! At your age?'

'I should have thought there was more good reason to go travelling at my age than at any other.'

We all slumped into silence. My mother and Kathleen cleared away the tea things. Gran and I sat where we always did, near the window, looking out at the great flank of hill that thrust away from the farm.

'Where d'you think you'll go, Gran?' I asked her.

'Oh . . . a long way, Jeannie. And when I get there, I'm going to stay.'

'Forever?'

She nodded. Her thoughts seemed far away.

'But where?'

'Maybe,' she said, 'it will be somewhere like India.'

Her voice was no more than a whisper, but it cut through the clatter at the sink and Marion's sweet singing and the stomp of my father's foot as he worked his way into his boot. For a moment it seemed as if even the kittens had stopped tumbling and the rowan tree outside the window had stilled the dance of its branches; and then everything lurched back into motion again as my mother swung round and Marion tipped down from her stool and my father stamped across to the table with his one boot tied and the other still in his hand, like a club to beat a child with.

'India! But you've never been out of this country! It's ten years since you were last in Sheffield, Mother!'

'Exactly!' And she sat, her mouth pursed in

that dignified and intractable way of hers, and refused to say any more.

The matter was not to be dropped completely, however; and as we walked back to her cottage, she and I, in what seemed to be sullen silence on her part, we stopped on the bridge and leaned against its old wall to watch the bright robin tugging at the grasses. The river, freshly swollen from the thawed streams, was rushing down from the peaks, and Gran said, 'I should be quite at home in India, you know, Jeannie. They have mountains there, too.'

'But why so far, Gran? And why forever?'

And even as I said that my mind spun round in a wild vortex like the river caught between the stones below me. Forever. That was a word that made no sense to me, like Death, and Eternity, and God.

'People think they know what's best for you, and they don't, d'you know that, Jeannie? The only harm you can do to yourself is to waste your life, and you can do that if you don't listen to your own voice. That's a terrible crime, to waste your life.'

'Do you think you've wasted your life?'

'I know I have.' There was no colour in Gran's voice, and no movement in her face. 'It's a terrible thing to come to my age and to say that. And you don't even know it's happening until it's too late. Not if you're listening to other people instead of to yourself. Don't let it happen to you, eh? Promise me that, Jeannie . . . that you won't waste your life.'

And I did promise her, though I was desperate to know how I could keep my promise, when it seemed to me that life would do what it wanted with me without giving me all that much of a say in the matter. And I felt as if I was saying goodbye to Gran then, with all that wild water tumbling below us and threatening to drown our voices in its noise.

My father had brought Gran's sister Jessie home in his trailer when I got back, and they talked about Gran all night. Why India, they asked a thousand times. Why India, of all places?

I sat curled in the deep sill of the kitchen window and watched the sky growing grey and the green of our hill deepening into black.

The mountains of India are the highest in the world, I thought. 'Land of poverty . . .' my dad said, '. . . and of mystics,' said Martin, '. . . and sacrifice,' said my mother. 'Jessie, you remember the talk the minister gave us?'

'The slide show of the Himalayas?'

'That's it. And he told us about the people he knew who were going out there as doctors and nurses and teachers . . .'

'He asked for money.'

'And he asked for help. We all had it in us, he said, to make that sort of sacrifice.'

Beech logs on the fire, and no other light, and no sound in the room above the whisper of the flames.

'Shame on you, Mr Curry, for putting wild ideas into an old lady's head!' my father shouted to the minister next day.

'Ah!' said Mr Curry. 'She's told you. I wanted to have a word with you.'

'We'll not hear of it, Mr Curry. We're not going to let her go!'

'But you see,' said the minister, but awkwardly,

because my father was scowling down at him from the back of our stoutest farm horse, and he was delicate in soft leather shoes on a muddied track, 'I've made good provision for her. I've done exactly what she asked me to do. You must trust me, Mr Tanner.'

'Trust you!' my father mocked. 'Expecting an old lady to make that sort of sacrifice!'

'But it's the only sort of sacrifice the old can make. It makes up, don't you see, for being old . . .'

But my father didn't want to see. He swung his horse round till her rump was inches from the minister's face, then cantered away with a huge spattering of mud.

Neither would my gran see anyone's reason but her own. She wrapped herself up in her plans, and would talk of them only to the minister. The weeks went by, and her cottage was sold to a family from the village, just as she wanted. She moved in with us for the last few weeks of her stay, and I surrendered my little room with its broad view across the valley and moved in with

Kathleen and Marion. Gran packed one bag with three changes of clothes, and kept it by her. 'I don't need anything else,' she said firmly.

And she gave everything else away. She gave my parents and Aunt Jessie much of her furniture, and her chiming clock to Martin. Marion had her shells that sang of the sea, though none of us had been there. She gave Kathleen her rings. And I had her chest of books, that had never been opened for fifty years or more. Kathleen was indignant.

'What a rotten present, Jeannie,' she said. 'You share my rings with me. Except not the moonstone one.'

But I wanted the books. I knew what was locked away with them, all those years. And I knew it had a lot to do with Gran's wasted life.

It was Mr Curry who saw to everything for her, though Martin could easily have done it all. He was always in and out of town. Nothing would persuade Gran herself to go into Sheffield, not even to buy clothes for her journey. 'What do I want with cities?' she asked. 'Noise, and cars, and people, and rush. What's the point?'

'Did you ever like going into Sheffield, Gran?'
I asked her. It was our last Sunday together, and
she was in the mood for telling tales.

'I used to love going in with my mother, when
I was a little girl,' she said. 'You know, my mother
was particularly fond of music. She had it in her
to be a singer, just like Marion here. There was
a young man called Lally, John Lally, and she
would go anywhere to hear him sing. He was
only a local singer, famous round about. I can
hear him now, like yesterday. But the best time of
all was when he sang in the lions' cage.'

Marion snuggled up to me, sucking her
thumb.

'They had a little circus, I suppose it was, by
the old tram shed in town. It was always there, as
far as I can remember. It was always there when
I went into Sheffield, anyway. And one day, this
John Lally took it into his head to sing to the
lions, inside the cage! He'd a voice so deep, and
so strong, that some said it would frighten the
lions to death!

'He sang his song, and they stood like statues,
and so did we. But what he sang that day, I don't

remember. I was too much agog with whether he'd be eaten before he got to the end, to notice what he sang!'

'Did you think he was brave, Gran, or silly?' Marion asked.

'Brave?' repeated Gran, wistfully. 'I'm not sure I know what brave means now. It seems to me that people must do what they must do whether it frightens them or not.'

'I think it was a terrible thing to do,' my mother said, not looking at any of us but at the sheets that she was folding and folding with great firm slaps on the ironing board. 'To take chances with your life is wicked. It's the only thing you have that you can call your own.'

But I was thinking that I'd have liked Sheffield if it meant that I could go and watch men sing in lions' cages there. I'm like Gran; I hate cities. Not like Kathleen. One day, I think, she'll leave the valley and go into Sheffield to live. But anyway, just before Gran was due to set off on her travels, she packed Kathleen and me off to Castle Market in Sheffield to buy food for her leaving party.

'I've no intentions of sneaking away without

a good send-off, I might as well warn you now,' she said. 'Though I've never given a party before. But everyone will be invited to this one. Except, of course, the Baxters.' And she said this with such a strange sideways look at Kathleen that I wondered what she could have found out that I didn't know, because there wasn't one person in our family who'd have wanted the Baxters at our party anyway.

Top of our shopping list was crab, though to my knowledge none of us had seen one, alive or dead, before. But that, Gran said, was no reason for not having them for the party, and if they were still groping round on the stall when we bought them, so much the better. And one was, of course; waving its claw at us as we approached, though I swear that the stallkeeper had it attached to her finger by a piece of nylon string. Kathleen clutched at her stomach at the sight of the horny creatures tumbling into my carrier bag and said:

'I've just found out. I'm allergic to crab meat!'

'But you've never even tasted it yet!' I shouted after her as she slithered over bulging fish-heads to get to the ladies' toilets.

The stallkeeper watched her go impassively. 'Can't stand crab meat myself,' she said. 'Makes me retch, easy as blinking. It's the cleaning of them,' she told me reassuringly. 'You can empty your insides out after a ha'p'orth of crab if it's not cleaned right.'

The sudden wild and terrible thought struck me that Gran was planning to give us all food poisoning so that she'd miss her train and not have to go away to India after all, and I put this to Kathleen as I helped her away from the sweaty smell of flesh and fish and fowl that stenched the summer's day there.

'Not even Gran,' said Kathleen, limply, 'could be that devious.'

The night before Gran's send-off party I was lying in bed, listening to the night sounds and the soft winds off our hill, when I heard my mother going past my door and up to Gran's room. I listened to their voices murmuring together, and after a bit I crept upstairs to join them. They didn't notice me at the top of the stairs, and I hesitated because my mother was sitting on Gran's bed holding her hand, and it seemed to me that maybe Gran was crying. I couldn't be sure. And I heard what she told my mother.

Gran looked very frail, and tiny, and I'd never noticed before how thin she'd grown. It seemed as if they'd swopped places, somehow, and as if she was a small child, frightened in the night, and being comforted by her own mother. I crept back to my room, and though I lay a long time looking out at the stars I didn't hear my mother come downstairs again.

But next morning Gran was as robust as ever, ordering us all about as we prepared the party. Trestles were laid out in the courtyard between the stables.

'What a smelly place for a party!' my mother objected, but it was the only place big enough to contain the invited, and the only place sheltered enough to keep us from the stares of wandering hikers. The eating was hugely successful, especially the crab meat, which Kathleen and I both assiduously avoided. My father, Martin, and several contemporaries of Gran's all made speeches, and the old walls of the farm seemed to bounce their voices back like an ancient theatre; and we hung our heads and listened, like any audience, and avoided each other's eyes. And then Gran made her speech, and said it was better than being at your own funeral, because you could listen to all the nice things your friends said about you and still tuck into all the grub.

She and Jessie sat apart in the shade while the trestles were cleared, and their voices rumbled softly like heavy bees in a summer garden till first Jessie, and then Gran, dropped off to sleep. At last the minister drove up the yard in his little black Morris, packed Gran's case into the boot, and woke her up gently. She jumped up, bright as a girl, and kissed us all lightly as if she was only off to Bakewell market for the day. Off she went, waving and smiling, waving and smiling, her little white hand pressed against the windscreen. All the villagers clustered down the lane to wave her off, and some hikers too, aware of occasion. The children from the school ran alongside the car, and Benjy, her favourite, waved the flag she'd made him years ago for the Jubilee. 'Bye, Gran!' we all cheered. 'Bye, Gran!'

And the little car gathered speed as if there was no time to lose, and the vivid sky and the dark hills pressed down on it so it seemed to be the centre of the world, that black speck of the car, and that tinier imagined white speck of Gran's waving hand.

I looked at my mother with Marion in her arms, and at my father with his hand on her shoulder; at Kathleen, and Martin, and Jessie, and I saw that the game was over at last, and that there wasn't one of us who didn't know by now that Gran wasn't heading for India, or for anywhere abroad for that matter, but for the little hospice just outside Sheffield where the incurably sick go to be cared for.

The stuffed fox

My Aunt Jessie's cottage was set a little away from the rest of the village, halfway up our hill, and down-track from our lane. It was said to be the oldest house in the village. It consisted of two tiny downstairs rooms of exactly the same size: in one Aunt Jessie cooked and ate, and in the other she slept. The walls were thick, and the sills of the mullioned windows deep enough to sit on. Her kitchen walls were covered with her little pen and ink sketches of the Peak District. A flypaper stuck with dead and dying flies spiralled in the draught her fire drew down from, and in the silence that welled in the room between talking, mice scrabbled in the upstairs room that no one ever visited. Hedgehogs came to Aunt Jessie's door for milk in the evenings, and village children brought birds with broken wings for her to mend. She grew wild flowers in her garden to attract butterflies and bees, and the scent of that ravel of meadowsweet and bluebells and wild garlic pervaded the house on a summer's day, heavy and heady as incense.

Aunt Jessie never used the upstairs room of her cottage, and nothing would persuade me to go up there as a child; because halfway up the stairs, where they twisted, a stuffed fox was mounted and met me with bright, cold, and terrifying eyes. I've never been frightened of live foxes, only thrilled by the way they sneak back into shadows when they're startled; but this creature, with its cruel fixed grin and its legs forever bent to spring, seemed to represent death most hideously.

'Aunt Jessie, why do you keep that old fox hidden up there on your stairway?' I asked her one day.

'Because I can't bear to look at it – ugly old thing that it is.'

'Why don't you throw it away, then?'

'I couldn't do that!'

'Why not?'

'Well, it's always been there. How could I throw it out?'

Later she told me that the fox had been a present from the man she should have married, had she not decided that she was fonder of her own company, after all. His trade was taxidermy, so if she had married him the cottage would have been full of the things – bits of fur making her sneeze, and legs and heads of creatures half-stuffed, and imitation eyes.

'No, I don't regret it one bit,' she said. 'But I was very fond of him, all the same. I couldn't give his nasty old fox away, now could I?'

In Aunt Jessie's house time stood still. Insects droned in the flowers outside the window, the river clinked as it curdled over clear stones, and the sudden high clamour of children's voices perked thinly across the field from the school playground, and hushed away again with the bell. Life was just as she wanted it to be.

But after Gran left she became listless, as if life had drained itself like the river bed in drought.

Every evening she had walked over our fields to Gran's cottage, or Gran had come over to hers, and they'd spend an hour in each other's company. We were all too busy to spend much time with her, and when any of us did call with eggs or vegetables, we made a quick dash in and out. I felt guilty about it, but once she'd enticed you to sit down by offering you a cup of tea, you were trapped. She'd a knack these days of making one story wander into another, so if you allowed your attention to drift you never found a convenient place to say, 'Well, I must be off now, Aunt Jessie.'

It was easier not to go in at all.

It wasn't surprising, then, that Aunt Jessie's loneliness made her depressed, in spite of her natural cheerfulness. 'The tick of that clock is too loud for me now,' she would say.

It was Kathleen's idea that she should take in a lodger. There were always people looking for bed and breakfast, at all times of the year – in fact they sometimes knocked at our door asking if we could accommodate them, which annoyed my father greatly. 'We're a working farm, not a holiday home,' he would say ungraciously. 'How would you like it if I came and knocked at your door for a night's lodging?'

However, Aunt Jessie was intrigued by the idea.

'After all, I'm much too good a cook to waste it on myself. And I'm spending so much time on my own I'll be talking to the teapot next!' We undertook to get the upstairs room cleaned out and repainted, and on the Saturday my mother took Aunt Jessie to Buxton market to get some bedding and extra crockery. By the time they came back the room was ready. All we had to do was to mention to a few people in the village that Aunt Jessie had a room for visitors, and wait. 'I'm so excited!' she kept saying.

I called by the next afternoon while I was out exercising Beauty. Aunt Jessie was sitting on her garden wall watching the late summer bees, and, I suspect, keeping an eye out for likely customers. As we were talking we saw a hiker coming down our hill, waving to us.

'Do you know her?' I asked.

'No,' said Aunt Jessie, shielding her eyes to get a better view. 'I'm sure I don't. But she seems to think she knows me, all right.' She bent down quickly, pretending to rummage through the flowers so that the hiker could pass by unembarrassed when she realized her mistake. However, she came right up to us, eased her brown rucksack off her shoulders on to the ground, and leaned over the wall to greet Aunt Jessie like an old friend.

'Hello there. I'm Winifred.' She held out her hand.

Aunt Jessie, flustered, wiped her soily hands on her skirt and looked at me for help.

The hiker stepped back to admire the cottage. 'Do you know, I've always wanted to live here. I came as soon as I heard. It's not gone yet, is it?'

'It's not for sale!' Poor Aunt Jessie was more flustered than ever, and patted Beauty distractedly on the nose, which is a thing she never does.

'The upstairs room, is it? Very nice! Lovely views?' The hiker looked at me sideways, as if trying to decide whether Beauty and I were part of the household or not.

'Have you come for bed and breakfast?' asked Aunt Jessie, trying very hard to be calm about it all.

'Bed, yes,' Winifred said, picking up her

rucksack and climbing over the wall. 'But I can't be doing with this breakfast lark. I suggest we share the cooking.'

Aunt Jessie signalled excitement to me. 'How long were you thinking of staying?'

They met at the door of the cottage, and seemed to sum each other up. 'How long?' said Winifred, hurt. 'For good, I hope. I've come to live here.'

Aunt Jessie's excitement mounted over the next few weeks. Winifred was no sooner her lodger than her companion, and no sooner her companion than her friend. She was the ideal person to share a house with: practical, energetic and full of new ideas; and the tactful changes she made seemed to be for the better. She re-arranged the sketches of Derbyshire to show them off to their best advantage, and even suggested that the less successful of them should be moved into Aunt Jessie's bedroom. She dug up half of the garden for a vegetable patch, and worked at it so zealously that Aunt Jessie gave up the hopeless and random plucking at weeds that had been her style, and actually undertook some drastic thinning-down of flower-beds on Winifred's advice. Children kept their distance because they could see that they were only a nuisance. At playtime and before the nine o'clock school bell the windows of the cottage stayed closed, so that the two friends could enjoy listening to the wireless in peace. Aunt Jessie, who had occupied her day by flitting from one task to another, found that everything was done by midday because Winifred had organized the household so well, and the two spent their afternoons striding the moors – Jessie always in her old blue raincoat, Winifred in her faded brown corduroys and her tan jacket, her red-grey hair wisping out from under her cloth combat cap. And they would talk, and talk, and talk.

And yet my parents weren't happy for Aunt Jessie. They didn't seem to like Winifred, though it was difficult to see why, and they wouldn't have mentioned it to Jessie for worlds.

'I don't know what it is about her,' my mother said. 'She's fussy. I can't stand people who fuss.'

'I don't like the cottage any more, the way she's

26

got it,' Kathleen said. 'It's too tidy. I used to like Aunt Jessie's mess.'

'I'll tell you what I don't like about the woman,' my father said. 'It's her face.'

'Well, it's not like you to go round noticing women's faces, John,' Mum said.

'You look at her next time. She's got a horrible face, that woman.'

My mother smiled at me, and I was dying to go and have another look at Winifred.

I called round one evening to find her curled up in front of the fire in the big red armchair, reading.

'Where's Aunt Jessie?' I asked, staring at her.

She didn't look up.

'She's in her room. She always goes about this time.'

'But it's only seven o'clock.'

'Is it?' Winifred was annoyed at being distracted from her book. 'She won't be in bed, you know. She has her own chair in there now. She'll be reading.'

I tapped on the bedroom door. I'd never been in that room before. Aunt Jessie was sitting in the little straight-backed chair that had been Gran's, with a blanket round her shoulders. She wasn't reading, just staring out of the window. She must have seen me coming.

'Are you all right?' I asked her.

'All right? Of course I am. Why shouldn't I be?'

The room was cluttered with bits and pieces of furniture that I recognized as Gran's, and with jars of wild flowers from the hedgerows. 'What are you doing in here?' I asked.

'Nothing. I like to come in here of an evening.' She looked at me knowingly. 'It's peaceful.'

'But aren't you cold?'

'No. No. Not yet. I'll get into bed when I am. Anyway, I can't get told off for making a mess in here. I quite like a bit of mess, now and then.'

'Does she boss you about a bit then, Aunt Jessie?'

'I wouldn't say that. But she likes things her own way. And to tell you the truth, Jeannie, I'm beginning to think I like things *my* way.' She mouthed this, as if she was scared of being overheard, and then said comfortably, 'But she's a very good friend.'

She seemed cheerful enough, but it puzzled me, and I resented Winifred's quiet smile and sideways look at me from her big chair by the hearth as I went through the kitchen again.

'Things are coming adrift,' said my mother, when I told her.

'Nonsense,' said Kathleen. 'They're friends for life, those two. One's as daft as the other.'

But my mother only shook her head, and sighed. And her worries were confirmed. Winifred pushed and pushed until she could push no further, and Jessie gave and gave until she could give no more. She was to be seen alone, stooping to pick armfuls of vetch for her windowsill, while Winifred's brown figure stalked the moors or followed the flapping lapwings across the fields. They worked together, in silence, each side of the tiny garden, and withdrew into their own rooms to eat the vegetables they had pulled. But the thing that finally drove the two friends apart was the matter of where to put the stuffed fox.

* * *

We were preparing for bed one evening when there was a rattling at the kitchen door. Kathleen opened it to find Aunt Jessie standing there with the grinning fox under one arm and her nightdress case under the other.

'What on earth are you doing here at this time of night?' my father grumbled, but Kathleen put her arm round her and drew her in to the warm.

'Don't, you can see she's upset. What's happened, Aunt Jessie?'

'We've had a sort of tiff,' Aunt Jessie said. She looked quite shaken, though she was trying to pretend that things were all right, really. 'I'm sure it'll blow over soon. It's nothing. It'll work out.'

'I don't know,' my mother said. 'You're like an old married couple, you two.'

'It doesn't *help* to be told that, you know,' Aunt Jessie sighed. 'She's very good to me.'

She shoved the fox under the table and sat down, looking at us as helplessly as we were looking at her. Kathleen brought her a cup of tea.

'I couldn't stay the night, could I?' Aunt Jessie asked awkwardly. 'I'm sure I'd manage on the settee.'

'You can have my bed, Auntie!' Kathleen said at once, but my father shook his head at her.

'Don't be a fool, Jessie,' he said. 'You move out of that house of yours and you'll never get back in. It's just what she wants.'

My mother sat down next to her. 'You know you can stay here. We'll help you, if that's what you want. But what happened, Jessie?'

Then Aunt Jessie told us how Winifred had taken the fox down from the stair-wall, and had put it in Jessie's bedroom. 'She knows I can't bear to look at the thing. I've told her often enough. But now she says she can't stand the sight of it, either – it gives her nightmares! I can't blame her. But how could I sleep with that thing gloating at me? And I can't throw it out – it's the only thing I've got to prove I nearly got married once!'

We all felt more like laughing than crying with her, but my father took the cup from her hand and fished her fox out from under her table. 'And this is your last chance to prove you still prefer your own company!' he told her. 'You go right back and put foxy-face back where he belongs. Do you know why old Winnie doesn't like him?

Because he's got the same ugly face as she has! Go and take a good look at her.' He led her out, and closed the door behind her.

'John! That's a bit cruel,' said my mother.

'It's cruel to be kind,' he replied, taking his boots off ready for bed. 'If she must act like a child, then she must expect to be treated like one.'

We ate our supper in silence, and I thought how sad it must be to be old, and without a real family of your own. I wished we'd spared Aunt Jessie a bit more time after Gran had gone.

First thing next morning Kathleen and I sneaked out and down the lane to Aunt Jessie's. I suppose we wanted to tell her that we'd have helped her if it hadn't been for Dad. As we went down her path the door opened, and out came Winifred with her full rucksack on her back.

'Looks as if I've outstayed my welcome,' she said. 'Silly old chump, she doesn't know what's good for her. Pity. Pity. I could have really made something of this place.'

And off she strode, without a backward glance.

Aunt Jessie was sitting at the kitchen table, sketching, with the remains of breakfast all round her and the windows wide open.

'Put the kettle on, girls,' she said. 'I just want to finish this off. Funny, I've had this idea for a sketch for weeks, but I couldn't seem to get going on it. I've been working on it all night.'

She's framed the sketch now, and hung it halfway up the stairs, next to that old stuffed fox. It shows a woman all in brown, thin-faced and sharp-nosed, with her back bent to jump over a stile, and her reddish-grey hair flying loose from her combat hat – looking for all the world like the red-grey tail of a fox.

And now wild flowers are beginning to thrust up through the vegetables in Aunt Jessie's garden, and children call, and the rooms are a-scatter with jobs half-done. We take it in turns to have Sunday tea there, and when there's a lull between talking you can hear mice scrabbling in the upstairs room where nobody ever goes.

Kathleen the city girl

My sister Kathleen is only two years older than me, but now she seems a whole generation away. We'd never needed friends because we always had each other; the nearest girl in age to me lived on a hill farm lower down the valley, and the nearest girl to Kathleen was only interested in horses, anyway. We did everything together: we shared a little flock of sheep, tended them and fed them and gave them all the care against infection that my father gave to his huge flock; and we had ten Rhode Island Reds between us, and the eggs from them were ours to sell. But Kathleen's thoughts were dragging away from these things now; I could see that, and it perplexed me because I didn't know what it was that was coming between us, or what I could do to prevent it.

But I knew for certain that she didn't need me any more during her last term at school. She stopped catching the school bus home with me, and every day I would walk back along the lane to the house alone, and wouldn't stop by the bridge to watch for the kingfisher, because she wasn't with me: and wouldn't climb up the banking to see if there were any new campers in Jones's field, because it was no fun on my own.

And she would come home late, having missed her tea and not wanting any, late for the walk-around that was her job every evening, and too moody to be bothered to swap a word with any of us. She'd go straight up to her room and come down again drenched in perfume and sparkling with the jewellery Gran had given her.

'And where do you think you're going?' my mother asked her, the first few times.

Kathleen would shrug. 'Over the fields,' she'd say, if she answered at all, and 'Like that!' my mother would reply, scandalized. 'I'm sure you're going to impress the sheep all right, with that muck all over your face!'

'It's not the sheep she's out to impress!' my father would put in. 'And if I ever catch her loitering round that campsite I'll turn the dogs on her.'

It was Kathleen's job every summer evening, just as it was mine before school every morning, to walk round the fields checking the sheep were with their lambs and hadn't got themselves tied up in any fencing; sometimes we did the two walk-arounds together. But not now.

'She'll end up in the city, you'll see,' my mother said. 'A tart with painted fingernails and coloured hair.'

'They're not all like that, Mum,' Martin said. He knew about city life; he was in and out of Sheffield every day. It didn't seem to matter to Mum, that, or if he came home late and sent all the hens squawking when he brought his motorbike into the yard. It seemed to me that things were easier for boys, all the way along.

One night I sneaked out after Kathleen to see just where it was that she was going all dressed up. I was so sure it was the campsite she'd made for that I went straight there, and hoisted myself up on the gate. There was a group of lads playing guitars softly and singing to themselves out in the warmth of the late sun, and I thought how lovely it must be for them, coming out to the valley and maybe seeing it for the first time. I sat on the gate, listening to their quiet voices for a long time. But Kathleen wasn't with them. And then I saw her, way up on the hill, making for the old cowshed, and I was so glad for her that she hadn't been hanging round the campsite that I stood up on the gate and waved.

'Kathleen!' I shouted. 'Kathleen!'

And 'Kathleen' shouted the lads from the campsite, in mockery.

Kathleen turned round, but she didn't come running down to meet me like she would have done once, spreading her arms to slow her speed and plugging the slope with her toes; shrieking with laughter. She stood, not moving, staring down at me, till all that distance away I felt ashamed for standing on the old cross-barred gate of Jones's field and prying into things that were no business of mine; or anyone else's for that matter. Would there come a time when I wanted to do things that nobody else in my family knew about, I asked myself. And I knew the answer was yes.

I went slowly home along our lane, where the trees hung low and the midges swayed, and the music from the campsite took up again; but whether Kathleen was still watching me or whether she had turned away to her walk I didn't know, because I couldn't bring myself to look up again.

My father was in a bad mood that evening: he often was. I sometimes wondered how my mother could stand his temper; his selfishness. But then I'd push the thoughts from my head, because it was wrong to hold such ideas about your own family. He'd spent all that day out in the fields with Martin, replacing a stretch of wall that some hikers had knocked down. This always made him angry. But he spurned the meal my mother had cooked for him – the piecrust was burned, he said, the gravy was too thin. She pursed her lips and said nothing. She was used to it. She put his plate back in the oven and took her chair opposite him. She would hear him out, and when he'd spent his anger on her, she would offer him food again.

'Did you finish the wall?' she asked.

He thumped his fist on the table, and I saw that his hand was powdered white and slit with cuts from the stones he'd been heaving all day.

'There's no finishing till the city louts take themselves back home,' he shouted, as if it was her fault. 'They wouldn't even use a stile if they knew what to look for. They're as narrow as the streets they live in.'

My mother raised her eyebrows at Martin, who'd finished his plateful and was looking round for my father's.

'Did you get Baxter to mend his wall?' she mouthed at him. He nodded, grinning. 'That's something, anyway.'

But my father started shouting again. 'I'll not mend Boy Baxter's wall for him, if that's what you're on about. I've pestered him with messages that his wall was down, and now he's roused himself at last.'

Boy Baxter was a sheep-farmer whose land shouldered on to ours just before it plunged away into the narrow valley at the clough. Boy Baxter he was to everyone, though he was a man of sixty and had boys of his own; but if my father mentioned him at all it was with a spit in his voice.

'Why do you hate Boy Baxter?' I asked suddenly. I don't know why I said that; nobody mentions Boy Baxter's name in front of my father. Kathleen was passing in front of the window as I was speaking: at least, I thought, it'll stop him yelling at her when she comes in, as he always did, it seemed, every night, until she cried.

Nobody spoke. Kathleen lifted the latch and came slowly in. She brought the chill of late evening in with her. I made room for her to sit round the fire with us. Upstairs Marion was singing herself to sleep, and the sweet comfort of her voice was like balm in all that silence.

'He's a bad farmer, and he's a bad neighbour,' my father said with bitterness.

'But his farm is the biggest in the valley!' I protested.

My mother shook her head at me, but I wasn't to be stopped now. 'You make us act as if we hate him, but we don't know why! I think it's wrong to hate people the way you do!'

'Hate,' said Kathleen gently, staring into the fire as if no one was listening to her. 'That's the ugliest word I know.'

My father's voice was quite steady, though his hand was not, when he lifted Kathleen's chin to make her look at him. I thought at first he was going to hit her. I think if he had done she'd have hit him back. 'If you want a reason for hating, hear this,' he said. 'Though I've pushed it down inside me for years and years.'

He dropped his hand from her, but she kept her face towards him, her eyes bright with ready tears.

'My farm and Boy Baxter's were the same size at one time – and remember, I inherited this land, just like Martin will. Baxter bought himself in. Now one spring, because he was a bad farmer, and a bad neighbour, he was too lazy to mend his broken walls or to notice that some of his ewes were diseased. And in one month, because his sick ewes wandered in amongst my healthy ones, I lost nearly all my stock. Wiped out, before they'd lambed. Or so sick they had to be destroyed.'

He pushed back his chair and walked across to the window, and stood with his hands deep in his pockets looking out at the sky, nearly black now, and the blacker hill below it.

'That precious campsite that those city louts of yours love to lounge in was my biggest field once. I had to sell it – Jones, Carter, Dakin – they all bought or rented fields off me to help me build my stock up again. And Baxter got away scot free. Wouldn't happen now – he'd have had the lot destroyed by government order, and so would I, to contain the disease.'

'But sheep are always passing things on to each other,' Kathleen said. 'Farmers share fields sometimes. You can't blame Boy Baxter.'

'I can count my losses against his.' My father raised his voice again. 'He lost six, and I lost getting on for two hundred. And I couldn't count the cost in unborn lambs. Now don't you go bringing any fancy politics in here, girl – that's city talk. I know what hate's about.'

Kathleen and I exchanged glances then, and she went quickly up to her room. I knew what her look said, all right. I bent down and re-arranged the row of sweet-smelling logs that were drying on the hearth. He's a good man, your father; a good farmer. I must always tell myself that: that was what my mother always said of him. But I sometimes wondered if he really knew, or wanted to know, any of us girls. Or if he cared about the way we felt about him.

When I went upstairs Kathleen was brushing her hair in the dark. I could just see the fine light of it in the moonlight. She whispered to me as I passed her door, 'Jeannie. Would you like to come into town with me one day? The first day of August? Will you come?'

I almost said no, it was so long since she had wanted to include me in anything of hers; but that second's secret glance by the fire had drawn me to her again.

'Won't you be working at the boutique?' I asked.

'I'm wanting to buy you a dress,' she said. 'School skirts and jeans for mucking out the cows – that's all you've got.'

I stood awkwardly, shy of her because of the notice she was taking of me. 'You'll be turning me into a city girl like you, Kathleen,' I laughed, and then stopped, because even in that dim light I could see I'd made her unhappy.

'Yes, I'll come with you,' I said. 'Thank you.'

I kept thinking about my trip to Sheffield with Kathleen. Perhaps she'd even start asking me to go in with her to the disco; though I didn't feel the need to get away from the valley like she did, I'd go with her for company. And we'd swim again, when the sun was warm enough, in the open-air pool. I never went there now, without Kathleen. When we were going into Sheffield on that Saturday for my dress I reminded her about the pool. 'We used to go every Saturday, and in the holidays every day, if it was warm enough. D'you remember?'

She was in a funny mood that day, all fidgety and giggly, and somehow I'd caught her mood, too.

'D'you remember that yellow costume?' she said, and we both exploded, so that people in the bus turned to look at us.

'I had a new yellow costume, you see,' Kathleen said, but she wasn't talking to me; she was talking to the woman sitting on the other side of her – someone she'd never seen before in her life. 'And we went swimming in the morning, and came back for lunch, and I put my costume on the privet to dry. And then in the afternoon we went swimming again. I went into the changing-room, and I put on my costume – oh, and I shrieked! Didn't I, Jeannie! I found a black thing crawling up my shoulder, and I pushed it off – and then there was another – oh, and then another – "Help!" I shouted, "Save me!" – and I pulled my costume off quick and threw it over the door of the changing-room. Do you know what . . . it was full of earwigs from the privet hedge! I can see them now, crawling all over me! I can feel them!'

Kathleen and I giggled all the way to Sheffield, and all the way to the boutique where she did her Saturday job. The morning sped in a crazy whirl of rush and laughter. One after another I tried on different dresses, and when I'd picked one she insisted that I kept it on, and on throwing away my old one – 'Out it goes,' she shouted, and threw it over the top of the changing-room door just as she'd thrown out the swimming costume full of earwigs. She bought one herself that had been put by for her for weeks. She looked lovely: a real city girl. We laughed at ourselves in the mirror.

Suddenly she said, 'Come on, we'll be late!' and we were off again, dodging the traffic, weaving through slow shoppers, with me a little way behind because I was looking at the new picture of myself in the shop windows and Kathleen combing her hair as she ran, till we came to a strange round building.

'This is it!' said Kathleen, and stopped. She leaned, panting, against the wall, and it seemed to me that all the colour had gone from her face.

'Where are we, Kathleen?' I asked. 'What's up?'

'Nothing,' she said. 'This is the registry office, that's all. Today's my wedding day.'

I'll never forget the way she said that, or the way she looked then, pale and young in the white cotton dress she'd just bought herself. What I remember most is watching a screaming child wrestling to free itself from its father's hand as it was led across the road. The child's screams stabbed through Kathleen's words.

'I want you to watch me being married.' Her eyes were closed. 'So you can go home and tell them what I've done. There's no way I'll be able to tell them. I don't think I'll be going home again.'

I stared stupidly at the writhing child, angry with it for its roaring. Why hadn't she told us? Why hadn't she told me?

'Was it a lad from the campsite?' I asked, almost spitefully.

'No, it wasn't!' she flashed. 'As a matter of fact, I met him in Sheffield, at the disco.' She smiled oddly. 'Though that's a laugh.'

So that was it. A city boy, just as my mother had predicted. A city home, with traffic, and shops, and bustle, just as she'd always wanted. At least it got her out of my father's way.

'If that's what you want, then,' I said awkwardly. 'Good luck.'

She nodded without saying anything, and I followed her into the building and into the office where her wedding was to be. I thought of our church bells ringing, and all the villagers clustered at the gate. I saw my mother and father smiling in their best clothes; and I saw them in the fields, grimly working, not knowing anything of this.

Some people were in the room already, acquaintances from Kathleen's boutique, come to be her witnesses. Kathleen sat stiffly on the edge of a chair, glancing from her watch to the door, away from me, away from anyone. No one spoke. My head was tight. One of the witnesses took off her shoe and peeled the price label from the sole of it.

At last the door opened and we all looked round. A young man came in and caught Kathleen's smile with his own. He sat next to her and took her hand in his. I could feel dread almost like panic rising up in me. I turned from the boy to the man who had followed him into the room; his father. And I knew him instantly to be the man my father hated; the owner of Daleford Farm. Boy Baxter.

My mother's story

I ran up the lane to our farm that evening, frightened to meet anyone in my new dress in case they asked me what I was all dolled up for, or wanted to know where Kathleen was. They would guess, I was sure. I could hear the throb of my father's tractor beyond the sheds, and Martin whistling. They were coming down for the meal. And it was that sort of evening when sounds carry, when the air hangs between the hills waiting for the rains to come.

I ran to my room hoping to change my dress before I could be seen, but my mother followed me in.

'Very nice,' she approved, while I fidgeted

with buttons, 'though when you'll wear it I don't know.' And she was gone to stir the gravy, leaving me regretting that I hadn't blurted out there and then, 'Our Kathleen married Alec Baxter today.' I'd paid dearly for that new dress all right – and it was typical of Kathleen to leave me to break the news. I'd be the one to be shouted at when my father found out. Why was it always Kathleen who got her own way, and me who had to do the explaining for her?

My father was in the yard already. I decided to wait until he went out again before I said anything, and to leave my mother or Martin to tell him, but Martin ran in with a piece of news that chased all thought of Kathleen from my head.

'A lad's come off the Edge!' he shouted through the open door. 'I don't know how bad he is, but I'm going straight up.'

'I'll come on with you, Martin,' my father called from the yard. 'Is he roped?'

'Don't know,' Martin shouted back. He was rummaging for his climbing boots in the porch. 'A boy came over from the campsite to tell me. I've sent him for the Rescue.'

Though my father and Martin didn't belong to the Mountain Rescue they often went out on a call if they heard about it in time. The Edge was on our land, but it was open access, and most summer evenings climbers could be seen clinging to the side of it like spiders on a wall, while the sheep lay above on the warm slabs watching them. Often, if anyone did fall, it was weeks before we heard of it, because the road was nearer to get to than our farmhouse if help was needed quickly. Martin was a good climber himself, though he rarely had time to practise it for fun, and my father, for all his rough ways, had an uncanny gentleness with sick creatures, animal or human. He found a walker once who had fallen and broken his leg up on the moors, and he stayed with him four hours till a stretcher came, just talking and talking to the man to stop him from fainting with pain. They set off quickly now, careless of the fact that both of them had been up and working since five in the morning. My mother put the meal back in the side oven, and sent me running after them with blankets for the lad.

It was just beginning to rain then, in huge heavy drops that seemed to have grown bloated with waiting. My father didn't send me back – he was too tensed up with preparing himself for what he might find, and so was Martin, and instead of handing him the blankets and running back home I stayed with them; not from any real sense of concern or even curiosity, but because I didn't want to leave my father then. We stood together as Martin pointed out the figure sprawled on a ledge some ten feet up; then we scrambled over the boulders towards him.

'Young fool,' my father muttered, but gently. 'He's dropped nearly forty feet. Not a rope. Not even a partner, by the looks of it.'

Martin lowered himself down from the ledge and came over to me for the blankets.

'Alive or dead?' my father asked, and I was chilled by the simplicity of the question.

'Alive,' said Martin, just as simply. 'Sorry for himself. He's only a kid. I'll not move him. They shouldn't be long with the stretcher.'

He went back with the blankets, and my father and I stood alone together again on the other side of the scree of boulders, looking up at the great dark Edge the boy had dropped from. Huge blisters of rain burst on dry earth round us.

'Cold?' My father looked down at me, frowning.

I shook my head, but he took my hands and rubbed them in his own.

'Your little frock's soaked through,' he said.

'Do you know about Kathleen?' I asked him.

'Kathleen?'

'She's living over at the Baxters. She married their Alec today.'

I still wonder whether he heard me. My voice was very low, and may have been drowned altogether by the sudden intense drumming of the rain. He moved off abruptly towards Martin and the boy on the ledge. 'You get home to your mother. There's no point in you getting soaked to the skin out here.'

'I couldn't stop her . . .' I wanted to stay.

'Go on!' he shouted. 'There's nothing you can do here.'

Marion and my mother were eating their meal when I got back to the house.

'Is he bad?' my mother asked.

'I think so.'

My mother shook her head. 'They think these hills are some kind of playground, those city kids. Young people – they're so careless with their lives. They throw them away. Why don't they *think* . . .'

We were picking at our food, none of us caring to eat properly, but my mother was more agitated than I'd ever seen her. 'He'll be all right,' I ventured. 'Martin said . . .'

'He's just as bad. Him and that blessed motorbike. He takes chances, just the same.' She shoved her plate away from her and sat with her elbows on the table and her fingers pushing back the skin around her eyes.

'They're having a party at the Baxters, Jeannie,' Marion said suddenly.

'Sshh!' my mother said.

I took my chance, again. 'Mum, it's because of our Kathleen.'

She shook her head, as if she didn't want to hear any more. Tears were starting in her eyes.

'What's it to do with our Kathleen?' Marion

asked. 'Why's she there, if we're not? That's not fair!'

'Go to bed, Marion,' my mother said softly.

'We should be there.' I tried to sound bright about it. Any other family would have been celebrating. 'It's our Kathleen's wedding day!'

My mother thumped her arm across the table with a force that sent Marion scuttling to the stairs in fright. 'I know. I know,' she sobbed.

Marion sat on the stairs, watching my mother doubtfully. I set about clearing the plates away. I couldn't do or say anything to console my mother. I'd have felt uncomfortable with my arm across her shoulders. Kathleen would have hugged her better, if she'd been there; somehow she'd have laughed her tears away. My mother cried often these days, often went quickly sad, especially since my gran had died. She told me, awkwardly, in one of these moods, that losing your mother was the worst thing that could happen to you, and that she'd found a depth of sadness within herself that she didn't know existed; yet so had I, and no one had comforted me. Now she caught my hand as I reached over for her plate, and whispered, so Marion wouldn't hear: 'I nearly married Boy Baxter, you know.'

I stared at her, my hand limp in her tight grasp.

'I wish I *had* done, sometimes, too. That's why your father hates him.'

I didn't want to hear this about my mother. The rain outside drove the boughs of our rowan down against the window; I watched the leaves flatten themselves against the pane, and I saw the passing shape of my father, with his face turned towards our light. I went over to the sink and stood with my back to the kitchen while my mother brought father's meal from the oven. He shook his wet jacket till the fire spat.

'How is the boy?' my mother asked. My father shovelled a big forkful of food into his mouth before he replied.

'Bad. Martin's gone along to the hospital with him. No one knows of him down at the campsite. Seems to have been a day tripper – watched some of the climbers, then decided to have a go himself. Silly fool. Lucky for him someone saw him come off, or he'd have been there all night.'

I shivered, thinking of the rain washing over the

boy's body, and him moaning quietly in the darkness.

'I hate to think what his parents will have to go through tonight,' said my mother.

'That's it,' agreed my father. 'That's exactly what your children don't consider when they do these daft things. They don't care how much they hurt you.'

I was watching them then, and I saw the look they exchanged, and as far as I can remember that was the only reference they ever made in front of us to what Kathleen had done. My mother sat down at the table, watching him in silence while he ate, and I followed Marion upstairs. I lay in bed listening to the rain drenching against the side of the house, until I became aware of their voices downstairs, his raised in argument. It seemed it was my mother who was to be blamed, then: not me. I tried to close my mind against them, and wondered if Martin was still at the hospital, keeping watch by the side of a boy he didn't even know, and whether there were still celebrations in Kathleen's new home. Then the door slammed and I heard my father in the yard, banging shut the door of the Land Rover, and driving off, with the dogs barking down the lane behind him. Again: silence.

I crept downstairs and found my mother standing in the porch with a coat over her head, watching the rain.

'Are you going out?'

She turned round, startled; a thousand miles away. 'Maybe I'll just slip across to the Baxters,' she shrugged.

'The Baxters? Now?'

She half laughed. 'I don't know. Maybe it's a bit silly in this weather.'

'But it's past twelve, Mum.'

'Is it? I would have liked a word with Kathleen.'

'Do you want me to come?'

'Yes.'

So we slipped out into the rain, and took the shortcut across the fields, but when we came to the clough that divided the two farms we saw that the Baxter house was in darkness. My mother stood a long time looking across at the dark shape of the building, while I shivered beside her and the farm dogs sent up lonely howls at our nearness. I touched her arm to draw her away.

'Well,' she said softly. 'That's that, I suppose. Too late to bring her back now.'

'Would you have done?' I felt a thrill of horror at the thought of my mother dragging Kathleen back home across the dark fields.

'I don't know what I'd have done. Maybe, after all, I'd have just wished her well. She knows her own mind better than I did at her age, anyway. That's something.'

Her bitter voice made me cold. I wanted to go back. I was glad I couldn't see her face.

'Why couldn't she have told me though, Jeannie?'

'I don't know, Mum.'

'That's what's hurt me.'

The day had been too long. I was too tired for all this. 'Where's Dad gone?'

'To Sheffield. He's gone to fetch Martin back from the hospital. He's long since missed that last train.'

'Martin can look after himself,' I said bitterly.

'Well, then. So can she.'

We walked slowly back through grass that was long and wet against our legs, and on to the stubble of the fields that had been cut down for hay. The sky was cloudy, and there was no moonlight. My mother carried a small torch, which was something the two men would never have done, and the light of it danced the earth a few feet in front of her so that we seemed to be always walking towards a point that leapt away from us into darkness.

I wondered if she wanted to talk to me about Boy Baxter again, but I had no way of asking her about him, even if I had wanted to. 'Kathleen looked really pretty today,' I said.

'I suppose she did.' The tone of her voice conveyed that she didn't want to talk about that, either, and drove us both into silence till we reached our house again. I went straight up to bed but she stayed down, doing the mechanical things she always did to keep herself awake when my father was out late, and then, I suppose, she fell asleep on the old red armchair in front of the dwindling fire.

Next day it was as if none of this had ever

happened. When I saw Martin he said that the lad would be all right, and that his parents had arrived at the hospital just before he left.

'Will you ring to see how he is?' I asked.

Martin looked surprised. 'What for? There's no point. He's nothing to me.'

In the same way Kathleen was brushed from our lives. No place was set for her at table, and no mention was made of her. My mother was brighter than usual, defying me, I thought, to ever bring to mind the conversation we had had. Just as the dry earth had soaked up all the night's rain, so the day with all its emotions had been absorbed.

My new dress was damp and crumpled on the floor, where I'd dropped it the night before. When my mother went out to do the yard chores I washed it through and let the wind blow it dry, and then hung it on the rail in my room, just in case I ever found a time when I would want to wear it again.

Martin's dilemma

Maybe Martin's story starts with a heap of smashed wood and ripped canvas, and he and my father facing each other across the room like strangers; or maybe it finishes there. It's difficult to know. What I do know is that the strongest ties that existed in our family were snapped on that day.

Martin was closer to my father than anyone else in the family was – we all knew that. It wasn't just a matter of sharing the farm work as they came to do when Martin was old enough – they admired each other's skills, and they trusted each other. There was nothing my father wouldn't let Martin do when it came to farm matters, and there was nothing Martin couldn't do when it came to farming. He was born to it, just like my father was. They were so alike they could have been brothers. It seemed they shared everything.

And I was jealous of that closeness. I can remember standing on the moor's edge with them; I'd walked up to meet them from the top field, and they were standing together looking down across the humped and bouldered fields of our farm, down towards the house and its neat white buildings. Martin was asking my father what he knew about wheat farms on flat land, orchards and the patterned fields that other men worked. 'Or other jobs? What else would you have done?'

My father shook his head, as if questions such as these were outside his reckoning.

'I only know this land, and how to farm it. What else would I want to know? There's nothing else I want – and there's not many can say that much. And one day it'll be yours – hey, think of that!'

And we all laughed, because of the well-worn phrase that always came close on that: 'But not till I'm good and ready, mind. Not before!' They walked away together; laughing, forgetting me.

There were five years between Martin and me, so I suppose there must have been quite a lot about him that I didn't know. He was moody, moodier even than my father, and when he wasn't out working in the fields he was usually in his room. He liked his own company, and we left him alone with it. It never occurred to anyone, not even my father, to ask him what he did up there all the time. But that evening, when they'd left me alone on the moor-edge, I went up to Martin's room to have a nosey round. And that was how I found out that he kept his ferret under his bed.

I hated that ferret. I'd been with Martin a couple of times when he went rabbiting with it, and it was weird and somehow fascinating to watch the change that came over him then. He would crouch down suddenly by a rabbit hole, tense and alert to sounds that I wasn't aware of; and with a kind of mechanical calm he would ease his ferret down and draw his net across the entrance to the hole. As soon as the rabbit bolted up and into the net he'd thump it across the back of the neck so that it would jerk with a shocked spasm; and then give up hope and drop like a rag, to be scooped up and swung in triumph across Martin's back. And I hated the look on his face, the tight line of his mouth, when he did that.

I saw him foxing once too, with a dog, and foxes are vicious things. Martin reckoned they would snap a dog's jaw off as soon as look at it. There was a cruel gloating in him when he told me this that I couldn't fathom. It didn't match with anything else I knew about Martin.

'Do you think that's fun, Martin Tanner?' I'd say, and he'd just shrug.

'It's neither fun nor cruel. It's nature, that's all.'

So when I discovered this ferret in his room, snuffling about in a cardboard box under his bed, I determined to get rid of the thing. What I intended was to set it free on the moors when he was out of the house next day; but some odd quirk of mischief in me turned that plan awry.

It happened the next morning, when my mother asked Martin to go into Sheffield to change some curtain material she'd bought.

'I've got too much work to do,' grumbled Martin. 'And anyway, that's women's work. Let Jeannie go in.'

'Jeannie would have to go on the bus,' she said. 'You'll be there in no time in the Land Rover. I'll hear no more.'

Martin pushed out of the kitchen, too cross to fetch the material himself, and my mother sent me up to her room to bring it down for him. That was when I remembered the ferret. I fastened down the lid of its box and placed it inside the carton of material, and carried it out to the yard. Martin was revving up the motor already, and as soon as I'd pushed the carton in the back of the Land Rover he was off. 'I'll shame him into freeing his ferret,' I thought. 'That's a better way than doing it for him.' And I went back into the house.

Martin, as I discovered later, was still in a mood when he arrived at the store. He carried the carton up to the fabric department and dumped it on the counter, handed the assistant the note my mother had written, and sauntered off to let her get on with it. She unfastened the lid, and out jumped the ferret. The girl screamed. 'A rat! A rat!' Martin turned and dived for it, the ferret swerved, darted through tunnels of legs and groping hands, sought sanctuary in bales of bright cloth, swirled through net curtains and sent stands toppling, until at last it found a roll of velvet cord and shot down the mouth of it. There it hid, trembling in a darkness that did not smell of rabbits but which was, at least, beyond threat of thrusting fingers.

No one saw where it had taken refuge, and Martin wandered round desperately, torn between wanting to placate the girl assistant, who was, despite her hysteria, prettier than any other girl he'd come across, and wanting to find his pet ferret. At last a little boy, who was the only person in the shop in the habit of squinting down tubes of material, recognized a blockage in one of them and declared loudly that the 'rat' was stuck. Martin and the floor manager were there in an instant. The young girl assistant bravely held the cardboard box over one end of the roll, on Martin's instructions. He whipped a piece of netting from the remnants tray and held it over the other end, like a bag. The floor manager, a blustering man who had never encountered so much excitement in his store since the day it opened, and didn't know what to do with it, loudly advised the circle of onlookers to stand well back in case they got bitten. He tilted the roll of velvet cord in Martin's direction. Out scampered the ferret into the net, and just as Martin was smiling triumphantly across to the girl assistant (who considered herself now destined to be his girlfriend) the floor manager stepped up, clenched his fist, and banged the ferret across the back of the neck. It jerked as if a new small spurt would save its life, and then sagged like a twist of cloth, unfolding into the piece of white net.

'There,' said the floor manager, nodding round to his customers. 'Can't have that, can we? That'll do, thank you. That'll do.'

I still feel ashamed about my part in that. Yet, in a way, something far more important came of that nosey round Martin's room – before I discovered the ferret. Because his table was covered in drawings – half-finished sketches for the most part, of sheep with alert faces, warm-eyed cows, the lovely soft curve of the fields below the bridge, the rough and tumble scattering of boulders in the top fields. I just couldn't believe that Martin had done them. I'd taken him for granted; without taking account of the complexities he had a right to; a quiet lad, double of his father; a scar of cruelty mocking his gentleness; a farmer, and a good one at that. And now I saw him as an artist.

The day of the ferret, when Martin came back from town, he slammed out of the Land Rover and set off on his usual walk: solitary at times like this, and rapid, with his hands thrust deep in his pockets. I knew where to find him all right. He'd be in the hollow of the field we call Deep Ditch, where the wind comes sharp as thistles and the winter fall freezes rock hard. I followed him there and sat with him while he told me what had happened at the store, and how the girl assistant had put his dead ferret back in the cardboard box and tied it up with string, as though that had been her way of saying she was sorry. And my way of saying I was sorry was to talk to him about his drawings, and to tell him I thought he should try to get into art college.

His laugh was scornful. 'Art college! What do I want with art college? I'm going to be a farmer!'

'But wouldn't you like to, Martin? You must know how good you are.'

He shrugged, shy of the compliment, just as I was shy of making it. 'You could do it at Sheffield,' I said. I'd worked it all out already, before I put it to him. I knew someone at school whose brother went to art college, and who still lived at home.

'Dad,' he said simply, as if that was an end to it.

'He'd get used to it. You could still help at lambing. You'd be off at haymaking. You'd be *here*, Martin. It'd just be the same as always. But think of it!'

'But I'm a farmer.'

'Martin! You can be two things at once.'

We didn't speak of it again, but some weeks later, when it was my father's birthday, Martin handed him a square of paper in a carrier bag. We don't go in for present-giving in our family; none of us can be bothered trailing into town, so we usually make do with bits of things we've fashioned at home and promises of better things to come. So, 'It's a drawing,' Martin said, and my father winked at Marion and pulled the paper out of the bag. Martin watched him tensely.

My father whistled softly, and held the picture up for us to see. 'Look at this, then! Our farm, hey? How's this for a present!'

I could see the care Martin had taken with this picture. It was our farm all right; the lovely white familiar building of it, the green swoop of hills behind it; the long low stone wall that runs down to where the river thickens underneath the bridge.

'*Your* farm, one day. When I'm good and ready!'

Martin laughed as though he'd never heard the joke before, and then said very loudly, as though he'd rehearsed it several times up in Deep Ditch where the wind was too strong for him to hear his own words: 'I'm going to learn how to do that painting in oils for you, Dad, and how to stretch a canvas, and how to frame it. Next year you'll have a real painting of our farm, for keeps. I've been accepted at Sheffield College of Art.'

And because birthdays loom up big and luminous I remember that it was exactly a year later that Martin gave my father the same painting, but oil on canvas, as he'd promised.

We were all sitting round the fire, and because it was a birthday it was a day of no quarrelling. As a special treat we all had a glass of elderberry wine, and I remember the sweet tang of it on my tongue, and how when I held the glass out towards the flame the red heart of it glowed.

'You did right to go to the art college, Martin,' my father said. 'I'm proud of you.'

It was the way Martin leaned forward in his chair, squaring himself, that made me look across at him sharply: and I realized that he was unfamiliar to me, now. When he wasn't at the college he was out in the fields, and when he came in he was in his room, always, painting till morning came. And no pleasure from him in anything.

'You *are* going to finish your course, Martin?' I asked.

He was silent for ages, it seemed. Swifts screamed in the twilight. 'Maybe,' he said, at last. 'But not in Sheffield.'

He looked at me, waiting for me to take him up, but I had nothing to say for him.

'What's this you're on about, not in Sheffield?' My father craned forward to peer across at him, affable because of the birthday present and the wine, not sensing, as we others did, Martin's misery.

'Well?'

Martin stood up so that his face was out of the glow of the fire.

'I can't do what you want of me, Dad, that's what it is. I can't work for hours in the fields, and still do my college work. Not properly. I can't do both.'

I could feel him standing behind me now, pushing the weight of guilt on to me.

'You can't do two things at once.'

'So,' my mother prompted softly. 'What are you telling us? That you want to leave us?'

But I knew that Martin hadn't made his mind up, and so did we all. He was waiting for my father to tell him what he must do.

My father stood up from his chair like an old man. He stood in front of the fireplace and lifted down the oil painting that Martin had made for him: our farm. He walked over to where Martin was standing by the kitchen table, holding the painting out.

Martin shook his head. 'No, Dad, don't give it back to me,' he said. 'It's yours.'

But my father didn't give it back to him. With the surge of temper that is so characteristic of him he swung the painting up and brought it down sharply on the edge of the table, smashing the frame and ripping a hole through the canvas. He picked up the bread knife and slashed into the fabric, chiselling into it as though he was trying to tear out the little white farmhouse in the centre of it.

'If this is what you think of my farm, then this is what I think of your painting.'

As I watched him I saw Martin's face in his; the grim line of cruelty that his mouth was drawn into when he'd chopped the life from those rabbits. I thought of the bid I'd made then to free Martin from this cruelty, when I'd wanted to set his ferret loose, and what the consequences of that had been. And I thought again of the evening in Deep Ditch, when I'd urged him to take that other freedom, the talent of his painting. Was I responsible for all this, then?

My mother stood with her hands to her face, but she didn't speak. Martin and my father stood like strangers in the room, with the shattered painting between them; then Martin spoke.

'I'll do what I have to do, then. I'll come back one day, to pick up the pieces of our farm. But when I'm good and ready, mind. Not before.'

The time field

In that last week before Martin left our farm my father's silence was broken only by bitter accusations of betrayal. 'A farmer needs a son,' he kept saying. 'You girls are useless to me.'

Martin kept himself away from all of us.

He and Marion and I had a last walk together up to Time Field, which had always been a favourite place when we were little. It had a stream that sprang from underground, lovely in the summer with water forget-me-nots and kingcups. Because of the way the fall of the land shouldered it on either side it was one of the most sheltered fields on our farm. The huge boulders at one end of the field were cast together in a way that looked deliberate, as if they were intended to provide cover of some sort, and we liked to believe that the first people to come across the Pennines from the west had settled there – and maybe they had. The air lulled between the two humped shoulders that hemmed it; it seemed to sleep. And in the far corner the ground sloped a little, and we used to say that that could have been a burial mound, worn smooth by the years. It pleased me to think of early settlers sleeping snug in the cool earth. I liked to think of children playing round those boulders hundreds and hundreds of years ago, and the dark hills holding their voices. I imagined a young girl just like me, sitting dreaming in the quiet September evening light, and that day my head spun with the notion that maybe I *was* that girl, and that what I saw and felt about the Time Field wasn't imagined, but remembered. Such ideas intrigued and frightened me, and I could never bring myself to speak of them to anyone.

I sat quietly by the boulders while Martin did some sketches to work on when he was away at college.

'You'll always draw country things,' I said to him, but he shook his head.

'I've never seen anything else to draw,' he reminded me. 'I've never seen the sea, or old cathedrals, or pit-head gears. It's all to be explored.'

'Are you looking forward to it? Are you pleased you're going?' I had hardly dared ask him before.

He shrugged. 'I suppose so. I wish I hadn't had to hurt Dad, though. I knew he'd take it bad. The farm means everything to him.'

'It means more to him than we do, that's for sure.'

'I can understand that,' Martin said. 'White Peak Farm has been in his family for generations. It would be terrible if it went to anyone else.'

It would be like losing touch with the past, I thought. That's how I always felt when I looked at the lichened boulders that may have housed families all those hundreds of years ago. It seemed important that the boulders should still be there. How could Martin leave it, I wondered. 'Do you think you will come back?' I asked him, but he just shrugged again.

'Here, you can have this picture,' he said, thrusting it at me. 'I've put you in it. You look right, sitting on those boulders. You look as if you belong here.'

Marion had followed us up to the field, trailing behind as she always did, and doing her own exploring. She called over now from the far corner, where the hill began to rise a little: 'Guess what! There's a great big hole over here!'

It looked fresh, as if someone had recently dug it, and went quite deep. When Marion wriggled into it, it covered her shoulders, and we had to prise her out. It was too wide for an animal to have made. Marion remembered seeing something inside the boulders, and ran back to them. She sent out two sleepy sheep, and came back to us dragging a spade and a pick.

'So whoever's been digging here intends to come back,' Martin said. 'That's a cheek.'

'It doesn't matter, does it?' asked Marion. She was all for carrying on digging. 'It's not doing any harm.'

'For one thing, it's dangerous,' Martin reminded her. 'A sheep could break its leg in there. Or you could, for that matter. And it's a cheek. You know what Dad would say if he saw someone digging up his field . . .'

'Bloody nuisance, the lot of them,' my father shouted when we told him about it at supper. 'How would they like it if I went and dug a hole in their garden, eh? It would just serve them right if I did.'

There's a local story that my father loves to tell us, about a farmer in the valley who found a day-trip family and their dog picnicking in a field outside his farmhouse. He was so angry about it that he demanded to know their names and address, and the next day the family found him and his wife and a Fresian cow munching away on the front lawn of their little house in Rotherham. That story is as much of a local legend as the one about the Tideswell farmer who sawed his cow's head off because it got stuck in a gate, but even so my father swears it's true, and I think secretly he wants people to believe that he was the outraged farmer.

He asked us to go back up to Time Field the next morning and make sure the hole was filled in properly, and to bring down the tools if they were still there. Martin finished his milking quickly, and I collected the eggs in from the chukky field, and fed the hens, and it was soon after seven when we set off. The grass was still stitched with cobwebs, with the dew still heavy on them, and the mist from the fields was barely rising, yet our digger was there already. We heard him long before we saw him. He was a boy of fourteen or fifteen, long and bony as a stick insect, with bright hair and big, dark-framed glasses. He grunted with effort as he worked, so absorbed in his digging that he didn't even notice us until we were standing right by the hole, and staring down with him at the crumbling earth. I knew I'd never seen him before, but Martin recognized him straight away as the boy who'd fallen from the Edge, all those months ago.

'What are you doing here?' he demanded. I think he'd have gladly pushed him down his hole if the boy hadn't looked so pleased to see him, and so innocent of the anger he was causing.

'Hi,' he grinned. 'I thought I might bump into you round here.'

'What the hell do you think you're doing?' Martin was not one to be distracted by friendly smiles.

The boy waved a thin arm, vaguely. 'Digging...' he said, trying to make a joke of it, and failing. 'Maybe I should have asked permission ...'

'Too right, you should. And you wouldn't have got it.'

The boy sighed. 'That's what I thought, really . . . that's why I didn't ask. But now I've started . . .'

'You can just fill it in again, and clear off.' Martin walked over to one of the boulders and sat down, arms folded, and waited. 'I'd have thought you'd have kept away from this place after what you've been through . . .' It's not really like him to be aggressive, not his style, but I think he was still upset about the argument he'd had with my father, which would never be reconciled.

The boy leaned moodily on the handle of his spade, scowling slightly against the light. 'I suppose he means it . . .'

I nodded, torn between indignation and pity. The boy lifted his spade back out of the earth and carefully drove the soil off it with the sole of his gymshoe. 'That's it, then.'

'What were you digging for, anyway?' I asked him.

'Does it matter?'

I shrugged and started to walk away towards Martin, and it was then that the boy told me what I had always hoped and known really, that it seemed to him that there had been an early settlement there, and that he was wanting to search for evidence.

'How do you know?' I asked.

'I just know,' he said. 'Look at it.'

'Yes.' I was allied to him against Martin, who was leaving the farm.

'I love looking up things about the past,' he went on. 'I belong to a society, and we visit all sorts of different sites. And now I've found this one. Nobody told me – I found it by myself. I was looking all round this field the day I had that accident. And then when I was in hospital I kept thinking about those boulders, and the way they'd been arranged – deliberately – just look at them – even with door-holes and chimney-holes.

And then there's this mound. You'd never guess what this could be.'

'I know,' I said, trying to keep the excitement out of my voice. 'I've always had a feeling about this field . . .'

But the boy wasn't even listening to me. 'I had to come back to see whether I'd imagined it all. And I hadn't. It's exactly as I remembered it. It's a settlement. I'm sure of it.' His glasses flashed earnestness, and as they winked in my direction and away again I felt my own eagerness rising. We ignored Martin, who sat at a distance, scowling, lost in his own thoughts anyway, and we walked round the edge of the mound, trying to define its perimeter, and to gauge the size and shape of it. It wasn't easy digging-ground, I was thinking. What I wanted most of all was for the boy to ask me to help him. But we came full circle, and he bent down dejectedly and lifted up his spade and pick.

'I was going back home this evening. I'd have replaced all the earth, and stuck the grass back in place. You'd never have known I'd been here.' He dragged his tools behind him as he walked away, allowing them to hump over the tufts of grass with a most desolate clank.

'Don't go!' I said, dismayed. Then, as he turned and Martin looked up: 'You haven't filled in this hole yet.' And then, with desperate inspiration: 'I'll help.'

The dip of the boy's glasses indicated that he understood me.

'Martin,' I said, 'do you want to get on with your packing? I'll stay here till he's put all this lot back.'

Traitor, I thought to myself, as Martin stood up to go.

'Right, I will. But you keep off our fields in future, OK? You know where the paths are. Stick to them.'

His voice rang with the bullying tone my father's had sometimes, and which I'd never heard before in Martin's. The farmer against the townies. 'I'm glad you're better, though,' he added, and went.

Yet he's leaving the farm, I thought. He doesn't really care about it.

The boy watched him. 'I'm fine,' he said. So much must have passed between them when he was lying in such pain on the ledge, and at the hospital before his parents had arrived. It must have been strange for him to remember that, and to put it alongside Martin's brusqueness now. Boys don't seem ready to talk about such things.

We set to work immediately, moving out in a line from the first hole, and digging to the same depth. We didn't speak. The day's heat intensified as the sun rose higher and higher. The drone of insects beat like a pulse. The dark soil shifted sluggishly where my spade pushed into it, and dropped with a thud as I tossed it aside. The boy grunted with every stroke of his pick. And still the sun rose, the crickets throbbed and the fat bees roared. My hands were wet on the rough haft, my breath rasped on dusty air, but while the boy was digging, I dug too.

We shared the lunch the boy had brought, and then we started again. I could hear the curlew on the high moors: cool notes clear as liquid. I could hear Dandy barking up the hillside, and my father whistling her, one, two, three times, rounding up ewes for dipping. I measured the thrust of my spade to the swing of the boy's pick and moved with him, inch by inch.

For a moment he stopped. He leaned on his pick and took his glasses off to wipe them on the hem of his shirt, and it was then that I found the brooch.

It was caked with dirt, of course, but it wasn't the shape of a stone, and I knew by the weight of it that it was more than just packed earth. I crouched down, trying to rub the earth from it on a clump of grass, and he came over and took it from me.

He cupped his hands round it as if it was a butterfly briefly captured. 'I was right! I was right!' His voice was thick with triumph.

Very firmly and carefully he prised up the dirt with his fingers. I watched the way the corners of his mouth worked, and how deep with satisfaction his breathing was. He seemed to have forgotten all about me. He sat with his long legs stretched out in front of him, and I squatted down beside him. Already I could make out some definition in the shaping of the object, and then the dull gleam of bronze, and in the centre of it, a red stone. He held it up so the sun glinted on it, and turned it slowly to change the depth of the red glow.

'It's lovely,' I said softly. 'How old do you think it is?'

'I don't know for sure. Maybe pre-Roman. Old. I really don't know.'

I'd been right then. Surely now my girl must have existed? Maybe this brooch had been hers . . . was mine . . . I took it from his cupped hands and turned it over and over, willing it to reveal something of the past. Who had owned it all those years ago? I breathed on the red stone, and rubbed it to make it gleam again.

'It's lovely.'

'You can't keep it, you know,' he said suddenly. 'I expect it will have to go on display.'

'But it's mine! I found it!'

'Course it's not yours. If it belongs to anyone at all, it's mine, because I told you where to dig . . .'

'I found it.'

'Only because I stopped to wipe my specs. Anyway, I want to give it to my society.'

'What society?'

'My archaeology society. I told you.'

I stared at him, too perplexed to speak. Our

moment of closeness was past; now history separated us. He held his hand out for the brooch, and I pushed myself away from him, refusing to give it up. I sat bowed over it, overwhelmed with weariness, and trying to understand it all. Tears of frustration were burning my eyes, but I wasn't going to let him see that.

'Come on,' he said, half-teasing. 'Give it to me. There'll be more finds like this, you know. Wait till I bring the society here and we dig up the rest of the mound.'

I suddenly realized what he was saying. Anger blazed up in me.

'Dig up the rest!' I shouted. 'Some crummy society! Digging up our field! You must be mad! My father would never let you do that.'

'He wouldn't stop us.' The boy's earnestness had returned. 'We'd get special permission. This could be an important find, for all we know. We can't stop now!'

The dark trench we had dug gaped like a wound through the bright grass. I heard Dandy barking again, and my father's whistled command. I knew what betrayal meant now, all right, and how much Martin and Kathleen's going had hurt him. The boy moved closer, angry himself, to take the brooch from me.

I suddenly scrambled up and away from him. I wanted to fling the brooch back down into the trench where it belonged and let the dark earth tumble back over it and close away its light for ever. The boy pulled me back and I shouted 'Dad! Dad!' I struggled free of him and ran towards the low wall by the stream. I could hear Dandy barking again, louder now, and my father came up and over the stile. There was no need for me to say anything. Dad stood watching while the boy collected together his spade and his pick, and rubbed himself down with the shirt he had flung down earlier. He walked past me, not looking, not speaking, and climbed over the stile. My father followed him all the way down the next field, and the next, till he came to the gate that would take him down the lane to the road.

And I still had the brooch. Later I would bury it again and mark the place so I could bring it back to light when I wanted to. But for the moment I sat on the boulders where the families had lived, and held the brooch to catch the sun, and thought about the girl who had worn it all those years ago and who had lived and died in the field that was my favourite place.

The hired hand

We were a house of secrets. We all of us kept our thoughts and our hopes to ourselves. Whether it's the way of country people, who count long hours of solitude as a way of life, I don't know. Maybe it was the effect my father had on us; his way of belittling our individuality. Either way, my gran's preparations for slipping with dignity into her brief, altered future; Kathleen's courtship leading inevitably towards family rejection; Martin's slow balancing of gain and loss as he weighed one sacrifice against another – they all showed a disregard or even a contempt for family consultation. My mother's secrecy was even greater, because somehow she bore the chagrin of my father's abuse of her without ever making a mention of it to any of us, and in a sense I think perhaps her silence on the matter reproved him far more than any midnight railing would have done.

But as for secrets, I think Marion's was the best kept of all. That she was missing, often for hours on end, never bothered us. She appeared at mealtimes, muddy from building dams in the stream, or purple-mouthed from picking blackberries in the graveyard, but she ate her food, and that was all that mattered to my mother. I never really thought about her – she was ten years younger than me.

One evening I stumbled on her, quite by chance, as I was doing my walk-around near the clough. I heard her laughing near an old shed that we used to keep equipment in, and I was just about to go up to her when I was stopped by the sound of a strange voice – a man's. Not Martin's, it was too deep for that, and anyway he was far from home. And certainly not my father's, because the speaker was telling Marion a story. I crept nearer and crouched down at the other side of the wall, beguiled by the low drone of the teller's voice. Occasionally Marion laughed or added something, and I could tell that she was speaking with her thumb in her mouth and her finger crooked to tremble the fine hair on her upper lip: lulled into a before-bed drowsiness.

Suddenly the story stopped. 'Off you go now, little Maid Marion, or your mother and dad will be fretting for you.'

Marion scampered off without noticing me, and when I stood up to see who the storyteller was he was moving away too, towards the equipment shed. He was blond and short, with a buckled leg, and his body arched backwards to balance him. Wilby Hodge, his name was. Will o'by Twist, we kids used to call him when we used to run away from him in the market place and chuck stones at him. And I hadn't seen him for years and years.

'What became of Wilby Hodge?' I asked my mother that evening after Marion had gone to bed.

She has a way of sucking in her lower lip when she's thinking, my mother. 'Wilby Hodge? Didn't they send him to be straightened out somewhere? Poor lad! And then his mother and father died, didn't they, and the place was sold up? But that was years since. Why d'you ask?'

'No reason. I just remembered him.'

My mother sighed. 'What would he be now? Thirty? A man.'

My father laughed. 'There's no amount of straightening would shape him up for manhood.'

'It's not his fault!' my mother snapped, and that was the first time I'd seen that flare in her. 'He's a better man than you, John Tanner, I'll be bound.'

'How do you know Wilby Hodge?' I asked Marion next morning.

Her eyes widened in surprise. 'Do you know him too? He's my best person.'

'But how do you know him?' I stayed her by digging my fingers into her shoulders, the way Martin used to do to me, and she squirmed.

'I'm not to tell,' she shouted, backing off. 'He's my secret friend.'

Marion was always having secret friends: lambs she'd helped to bottle-feed; the one-eyed dog who roamed the campsite; the hedgehog that lurked in the milking shed – these were part of the fantasies she peopled her private world with. I shrugged Wilby Hodge off with the rest of them. And the next time I thought about him was one drab evening in late October.

My father had gone out in the afternoon, off to the top fields to do some wall mending. He'd shouted at Marion on his way out for some small offence she'd committed, and she'd run off crying into the sheds, leaving my mother and me alone in the house.

'Peace and quiet, with him out of the way.' She'd laughed, but I knew she meant it, then.

By teatime it was growing dark, and she was peering through the windows again and again to watch for him coming home. 'I don't like him working the tractor in this light,' she said. 'Especially in those top fields.'

'He can read them like a blind man,' I said, quoting him.

'Well, we'll eat,' she sighed. 'Fetch Marion, will you?'

But Marion wasn't anywhere around the house.

'Find her,' said my mother. 'It's nearly dark.'

'How do I know where she is?' I shouted. We were both edgy as rabbits, and it was something to do with the effect the breathlessness of that coming night had on us; the way the animals had stopped their shouting, and the way the strange gloom of the sky had merged into the fields and into the hills.

'Perhaps she went out with him . . .'

'Not with *him*,' I said scornfully. 'What time does he have for her?'

'Then where, at this time of night?' – shouting, but shrill, with an edge of fright in her voice.

And then I remembered. 'Wilby Hodge.'

My mother grabbed my arm. The grip of her hand hurt my wrist.

'Where is she?'

She dragged me out of the door. She had my father's house-shoes on, and they were too big for her. I remember that, and the way her heels swung over the sides of them and bit into the stony track as she ran. Without realizing it even, I took the lead and pulled her over to the wall by the equipment shed where I'd first spied them. I could hear the slapping of my mother's feet, and the way her breath snagged in her throat, and then I heard another sound: a thudding and dragging, uneven sprawl of a run, and I knew that it was Will o'by Twist coming, and that he was on his own.

'Where is she?' My mother fastened on to his arched shoulders as if she would pull him forward in spite of himself.

Wilby's eyes were nearly out of his head with fright. 'She's with her dad. She's in that field with the dips.'

Deep Ditch. Ribbed like a dead man's chest.

'You'll have to send for help, Miss,' Wilby blurted out again.

My mother pushed him out of the way and started up the steep track that would bring her a good hour later to the high field, where in a hollow my father lay with an overturned tractor across his legs and Marion whimpering beside him.

That terrible night preceded some of the best weeks we were ever to know on our farm.

I phoned the warden and an ambulance, and somehow they got my father down from the hill and into the hospital in Sheffield. It seemed hours before my mother and Marion came back to the house, and we sat up till nearly light, too tired and shocked to sleep. Marion told us how she and Wilby had heard my father shouting, and how Wilby had struggled to pit his poor body against the tractor to lift the weight of it from my father's leg.

'Why were you with him, though, Marion?' my mother asked. She was sunk forward with her hands pressed against her chin, and her hair loose across her face. 'Why does he skulk around here?'

'He's run away from his hostel,' said Marion. 'They gave him a job making soap. But he doesn't like town work.'

'So he came back here.' Mother sighed. 'But he hasn't got a home here now. That poor child. That poor child.'

'A man now,' I almost said. I remembered suddenly the last time I'd seen Wilby before he was sent away. I remember we'd all been splashing about in the pool, about a dozen of us kids from the primary school, with my mother and my gran watching us. Wilby had come down to the water's edge too, and then all of a sudden he'd lurched forward, fully dressed, stumbled with his strange arched swagger, his chest thrust forward and his arms swinging back to balance himself, right down and into the water. We kids had all run screaming to the side. He thrust himself out with long strong strokes, and we watched him bring himself powerfully across the pool, backwards and forwards, tossing his head and snorting water from his mouth, laughing across to us.

'What a fine man he looks now!' my mother had said.

'The water is his element,' said Gran.

The morning after the accident my mother sent Marion and me to look for Wilby. He was sleeping in the equipment shed, on a bed of old sacking and straw. Although I found it hard to look at him, Marion slipped her hand simply into his and skipped beside him down to the house. My mother had cooked a meal for him just as she cooked breakfast every morning for my father, and he ate it as if he'd been expecting it.

'They say my husband will be in hospital for some weeks, Wilby,' she said, and her voice was level. 'If you can help us out here, we'd be grateful.'

Wilby was wonderfully strong and patient with the animals. We brought all the ewes down for tupping and this year's lambs for dipping. He and my mother went to the market together and defied the wondering looks that were cast on them. He brought the older ewes down to the home fields for winter, and set up a good store of food for them. He advised us without seeming to, and was gentle in challenging our mistakes. We all loved working with him. And in the evenings we closed round the ash fire, and Wilby told us about all the years he'd passed in hospitals and homes.

'Why did you hate your factory job, Wilby?' my mother asked.

He laughed. 'I tell you – if you're born a different shape to other people, they don't know what to do with you. It seems that because I can't fit into their clothes, so I can't fit into their heads, either. The only way you can manage is if I act as if I know my place. That's not easy, you see. They don't understand me. Or won't. Well, the people at the hostel found me a job, and they told me how lucky I was to get it. I went in that first day, and the woman in charge came up to me and said – only she didn't say, she shouted, as if I was deaf – "I'll make you a special overall." So I shouted back, "You don't have to, I won't spill my dinner all down me." I meant that as a joke. She walked off, and another woman came, and she shouted at me too. "Now, we're going to sit down here, aren't we, and watch what these ladies do. And then we'll have a go, won't we?" I nearly walked off then, but I remembered what they'd said at the hostel, about how lucky I was to get the job, and besides, I was determined to let these women see I could do it as well as them. But they were determined I couldn't. They kept hovering over me and trying to do it for me, and asking if I was all right and saying "Isn't he doing well!"

'What I had to do was this: I had to pick up six bars of soap at the end of a conveyor and stack them on a tray. They said to pick up three in each hand if I could manage it – and of course it jumps out of your hand at first – but after a bit I found I could do it quite easily, in fact my hands were so big I could pick up four easier than three. I was really pleased with myself. I was picking up eight to their six – I could work faster than them!

'Then one of the women screamed out: "He's going too fast! Look what he's doing! He's picking up the soap too fast! No love . . . you don't do it that way. You've got it all wrong. Let me show you again."

'That was it. I picked up all the trays of soap that I'd stacked – that they'd spent all day stacking, stacking and stamping and wrapping and sticking pink plastic free combs on, and I tipped the whole lot back on to the conveyor belt, so it all piled up at the end and squidged together and mangled into the boxing machine and then started spinning out across the room with pings of plastic and shreds of wrapper and the women were all shrieking at once. And then I ran for it.'

My mother poured wine for us on these nights, and the room was warm with laughter and storytelling till we climbed up to our beds and left Wilby to fold himself as best he could on the long couch by the fire.

They brought my father home in an ambulance, nearly a month into the New Year. His skin was pale with being out of the weather for so long and, he grumbled, from too much washing. They lifted him down from the ambulance into a wheelchair, and my mother brought him into the room. Marion and I stood silently by the door. My mother and the ambulance man rolled him from the chair on to the couch we'd come to know as Wilby's, and we watched the pain flash across his face as he was moved, and saw the strange angle they tucked him into before they drew the blanket over his body.

My mother lifted a chair to sit beside him. 'At least you're home, John.' Marion and I crept about preparing the meal. He seemed to sleep.

And it was Wilby who wakened him, stomping into the kitchen with his familiar dragging stride, shouting to Mother that he'd got the old tractor going again, holding out his hand for Marion to run to him. He stopped short when he saw my father, and my father opened his eyes and looked from Wilby to my mother, and then to us girls, and back to stay fixed on my mother. The reproach in his silence burned into me like a flush of shame.

Wilby took off my father's jacket, that Mother had given him for working in the fields. I saw how the arch of his back had pulled out the shape of the shoulders. He picked up his own bundle of clothes that had been moved from the couch to make room for my father, and I watched how he had to bend sideways to do it, how he had to thrust one leg out for balance. I think I hadn't noticed that for weeks.

He stood awkwardly in the silent room.

'I think I'd better go now mester's come,' was all he said, and not one of us had anything to say to keep him there.

Woman farmer

We were a farm without a farmer, or so my father said as he lay week after week on his couch of sickness by the fire, watching the winter through the window. Though it wasn't true. He wouldn't acknowledge it, but the farmwork was done in spite of him. I did my bit when I came home from school at nights, and sometimes I took days off when it was needed, and that was never questioned; but it was my mother who did the great part of it.

By Easter he was beginning to move round a little on crutches, but he never left the house. Gloom settled on all of us. We recognized his depression and, to some extent, his resentment, but never talked about it. We just let him get on with it, I suppose, ignoring his complaints, while he unwillingly let my mother get on with the business of running the farm.

After lambing there was to be a dance at the village hall. We had one every year – the Easter Ball, we called it, and it was something all the local farming people and villagers looked forward to, a way of coming together again after the hard months. I especially looked forward to this year's – we seemed to have been locked into our farm for weeks on end. But my father scowled when I came downstairs in the pale dress Kathleen had bought me last summer for her secret wedding.

'Where d'you think you're off to?'

'You know very well where I'm off to. Easter Ball.'

'Well, you're not to go. There's work to do.'

'It's done.'

'And the weather's turning. You're needed here.'

'I'm going to the Ball.'

I escaped from that oppressive room of guilt and shame, and stood outside listening to his voice taking up again against my mother. 'Pig! He doesn't deserve her!' I was glad of the cool touch of evening air as I made my way down our lane towards the village and the winking lights of the decorated hall. You could hear the band from fields away. It never got any better, from year to year, but it always brought a gypsy thrill to hear it. The bandsmen were begged and borrowed from villages round the valley and learnt or remembered their music during the course of the evening's play – the sax player never achieved the same key as the accordionist, though neither seemed to mind. The drummer now ached to play heavy metal, and played with his eyes cast up to the cobwebbed ceiling. The bass-player battled with feedback. The one constant was the second cornet from the village band, who never forgot that he was good at playing marches. They were at one in their brash, determined gaiety, and at odds in tempo, key and melody; and it was wonderful to hear them, and to be beguiled by them from our cottages and our farms, all in our shy best clothes.

* * *

By the time I arrived some of the already tipsy were setting the pace in a whirl of romance, in the unlikely and outrageous poses of the ballroom. Women clutched their handbags still, and their partners pressed close, eyes shut, hands primly correct, humming the melodies that evoked their youth. We girls laughed and pointed till we dared each other to dance, too, and then we taunted the village lads. We aped our mothers' steps, and that made us laugh the more, disciplining ourselves to try the strange marionette stagger and sway of the ballroom dance.

I was pleased when my mother came down in her flowered summer dress and her soft linen shoes. She danced with her sisters, and later with their husbands, and her face was red with the laughter and the exercise. Marion skipped hand in hand with the other little children, interrupting the solemn business of the grown-ups' dancing. I knew every soul there.

The baffle of talk and laughter and hurdy-gurdy music swilled round me, and I suddenly thought of my father lying alone on his couch by the fire, maybe hearing it all too from all that distance away, and for the first time I pitied him. I slipped off home away from the light and the noise into the night's new darkness and I let my face into the ugly shape of grief – for him and his pain and his loneliness; for the blackness in him which divided him from the rest of us and us from each other; for my mother, who somehow had to bear the brunt of it all and who was now out enjoying herself dancing the quickstep with her sisters' husbands.

I couldn't tell him I'd come back on his account. I sat on the hearth near him, not knowing whether he was asleep or awake. You could hear the sounds of the ball, drifting up like the waves you hear in seashells.

'Is your mother there?' he said, and that was all.

During the night the wind got up. I heard it like a voice at first, in the swoop of branches from our tree; and then from the hill behind the house it took up a howl that shot me from my bed. Things were slamming round the yard, animals were crying, and I stood bewildered by my window, trying to focus on the centre of the tumult. Then I realized what it was – the roof had blown from the lambing shed and ewes and lambs were screaming for their lives. I ran to my mother's room. She was sleeping on the top of her bed, still in her flowered dress and linen shoes, and dreaming sweetly. I pulled her awake and we ran downstairs past my father and out into the shriek of the wind.

Mother dragged an old tub across the yard and scrambled up on to the top of the shed roof, her flowered dress billowing round her. The door of the shed slammed brutally backwards and forwards as frightened ewes tried to stagger through it, and I abandoned the effort of trying to pin it back for them. I dashed into the shed, and with my mother leaning down dangerously and heaving from above and me pushing from below, we managed to prise up the beam that had crashed down across the pen where new-born lambs lay in the warm straw. Frightened ewes huddled together, terrified for their young, and, in a bundle, charged me in the darkness.

The most we could do was to carry the lambs

into the kitchen. I dropped a couple into the pockets of my coat and stumbled out through the press of rushing ewes and the threat of the heaving door. The kitchen light was on. My father trundled out in his chair and held the torch up for us, then parked himself against the swinging shed door. Things were easier then. We removed all the loose wood so no more harm could come to the animals, and bedded the ewes down in the cowshed, empty of stock since Martin left home. But the wind still tugged and raged and now there was the harsh touch of gravel in it. My mother knew what it was.

'Bed,' I said, when the last of the new lambs were settled. But she shook her head.

'Not yet. There's snow in the wind, Jeannie.'

Easter snow. It had happened once before, I remembered. It stayed three days and we lost one hundred and eighty lambs. Many of the lambs were up in the fields already.

'We could fetch them down in the morning, when it's light,' I said.

My father was wheeling himself back to the house.

'You will not,' he said. 'They'll be dead by then.'

* * *

It was dawn before I got to bed. The snow had come in with the wind, and as the wind abated the snow thickened. My mother and I made our way in the thick of it up to the moors, and brought sheep and lambs down from the top fields towards the farm, to be as near to the house as possible. The snow had come so quickly that already the top fields were covered. Martin would have known where to find the sheep; we didn't. We remembered where the hollows lay and searched in them first, in case they had gathered there in their panic. My face was sore with the slap of the cold and my fingers were numb. My legs ached. My mother made me go to bed at last but she worked on, trailing with the dogs from field to field, carrying bales of food up ready. The snow might last for days; the sheep in their terror might go anywhere.

I woke suddenly to the cold dead world the snow presents. I stumbled downstairs. My father was where I had left him, watching through the window for my mother to come back in. Neither of us spoke. I ploughed back up the track, past the abandoned tractor. Then I saw three figures standing in the home field, with the bulk of our flock gathered round them, brought down to safety. It was my mother, and with her were my sister Kathleen and her young husband Alec from over the fields on Baxter's farm.

'We've done!' my mother called to me. 'Thanks to these two. Will you come in now, Kathleen, and talk to your father?'

Kathleen hadn't been inside our house, or on our land, since she married Boy Baxter's son. She shook her head.

'I think we might be wanted back on our farm, now.'

I hated that, and so did my mother, I could see that. 'Our farm'.

'Well then,' said my mother, as she would to any farmer who had come across to lend a hand. 'I'm grateful for your help.'

We walked back to the house together, and I saw that my father was still craning to see us through the window. When we came into the kitchen he had wheeled himself back to his couch.

'What did I tell you! I knew this would come!' he said.

By the end of that week most of the snows had gone. My father never spoke to my mother about it, and she never complained about the night she'd had. He took to his couch again, and made no effort to heave himself about on his crutches. You would think the farm didn't exist – my mother did the work, and said nothing: never asked his advice, or his approval, or his wishes, and he never gave them. She or I cooked for him still, and sometimes he ate it, and sometimes he didn't. There was no talking in our house now, not even between my mother and me. His gloom seemed to settle on everything, like the deep dust that shrouds a room when it's no longer cared for. There was no living in the place.

At the weekend I walked over to Boy Baxter's farm and asked to speak to Kathleen. She was queening it in their kitchen, surrounded by all the men-folk of the Baxter family, ordering them about and giving them jobs to do.

'What's happened?' she said, when she saw me. 'Is my father worse?'

'As bad as he'll ever be,' I said. I felt now as if I wanted to sink down into one of their big fireside chairs and sleep, with all that kitchen bustle and joking round me. 'He's terrible, Kathleen. He's draining the life out of my mother with his misery. It's not right.'

'What can she do?'

'She should leave him.'

Kathleen laughed. 'She couldn't do that! What about the farm?'

'Say she lived in Aunt Jessie's house,' I suggested. 'She could come over to the farm every day from there.'

'What about him?'

'He can fend for himself, if he has to . . .'

Kathleen agreed. 'I suppose he could, then.'

'Will you come to talk to her with me?'

'I couldn't!'

'Please, Kathleen!'

'I don't know.' She turned away. 'I don't think we've the right.'

'It's all right for you!' I argued. 'You got out!

You found a way!'

Alec came over and put his arm round Kathleen. 'I think maybe your mother is bringing it on herself,' he said, 'if she's making him feel she can do everything without his help. What can he do?'

I was amazed that Kathleen could let Alec say that about my mother and not rebuke him. I wouldn't hear anything said against my mother.

'So you won't come with me?'

Kathleen had turned back to her work, paring vegetables, with Alec helping her. 'She chose to marry him.'

'She didn't choose to marry a cripple!' I wished I could have taken those words back – I felt a terrible sense of disloyalty even to my father in saying that. But it was true; he was a cripple. The vigour was drained from him, maybe for ever.

Kathleen was watching Alec as he carried the vegetables over to the sink to wash them. 'I think the choice is still for her to make, Jeannie. Not us.'

I went back knowing I was on my own. I walked about till nightfall, turning the ideas over and over in my head. I would speak to my mother tonight, I decided, and help her to break away from the tyranny. I would speak to them both. That was the way. Tomorrow I would go to Aunt Jessie, and talk to her about taking us in. My father would have to fend for himself. I knew I was right, and the relief of it made me run at last across the fields towards the one warm light from our kitchen. Maybe tonight was the last night I would ever sleep in the house.

I stopped as I came to the door. There was music. I walked round to the window and looked in. The music was coming from the record player that hadn't been touched since Martin left home. It was a dance-band waltz – one of my father's old records. My mother was wearing her flowered summer dress and her linen shoes, and my father was standing, propped up by her. They weren't dancing, but swaying, hands clasped, arms round each other's waists. They both had their eyes closed. I opened the kitchen door and tiptoed across the room, opened and closed the further door and crept upstairs, while the dance-band waltz played on. As far as I could tell, they never heard me.

Jeannie leaves home

Late May, and a sky like polished birds' eggs, so clear it seemed to have a roof on it; and always somewhere up there the lark, churning and churning like a ring of bright steel twisting. My last summer at White Peak Farm.

Exams were looming close for me, but it was hard to bring myself in at night from my walk-around in the fields. I liked to be right up on the moor's edge, where the dogs would send up the startled grouse and the curlews would cry and over the valley below me the brown kestrel would lie on the wind. Sometimes I'd meet with my sister Kathleen at the clough which divided our two farms, and these days she would walk down with me to our house, and we'd take a last hour in the yard with my mother, talking. My father would be in his chair in the kitchen doing the books, and he and Kathleen would wave to each other courteously enough, though she would never be invited in. I'd leave them reluctantly and go up to my room and look out at the tree dancing its diamonds of light across the window. I would sit with my notes in front of me and listen to their voices, and Marion chattering to my father in the kitchen. I could hear the lambs bleating across the fields to each other, and the beasts in the sheds lowing. I could hear the flutter of hens in the yard; and still the lark: churning, churning.

My favourite teacher at school was Mrs Kennedy. It was because of her that I was giving so much time to my studying. I had special lessons with her in the lunch hours. There was nothing we couldn't talk about; sometimes I felt she knew me better than my own mother did.

'What will you do after the summer, Jeannie?' she kept asking me. I knew she meant after my A Levels, when I'd left school.

'I'm to help my mother on the farm,' I said.

'You want to be a farmer?'

I laughed. 'No, of course I don't.'

'You want to marry one, then?'

'No. Oh no!' Never to live in someone else's farm. And marriage? I hadn't even thought of it.

'I'd like to come and have a talk to your parents,' she said. 'Can I?'

I was in an agony about her coming. I thought she might come in her loose Indian dress and sandals and look ridiculous out in the field where she would have to be if she talked to my mother. I thought my father might stand shouting to her from the kitchen door, leaning on his crutches, refusing to let her in; not calling off the dogs.

'If you have to,' I shrugged. 'Must I be there?'

She smiled. 'Of course you must. It's you I want to see them about.'

My mother came down from the thistle field when she heard the car in the drive and the dogs starting up. My father was propped up on the couch, and although he didn't stand, because to do so would have meant a struggle with crutches and a humiliation for him, he was affable enough. I made tea, and all the time I was conscious of my working jeans and the frayed carpet, the damp clothes steaming on the rack; the cats scratching themselves in the doorway.

'I'd like Jeannie to go to university,' I heard Mrs Kennedy say. 'And I thought perhaps she might not have asked you.'

'She's had two more years at school than her sister,' my father said. 'Isn't that enough?'

He didn't even mention Martin, his favourite, who had given up farming to go to art college. That scar was still too sore for him to touch.

'What point is there?' my mother asked. 'It's wasted on a woman. I still think that.'

I listened to them all, turning it all over and over as if I wasn't even there, and I thought, 'Is it really what I want?' I didn't know. I wanted to please Mrs Kennedy.

She won them over in the end. All I had to do was to win the place at university – maybe at the Oxford college my gran had been to. Mrs Kennedy wanted that, at least.

'It won't mean anything to them, you know,' I told her, during one of our lunchtime sessions.

'Well, it will to me,' she said.

It was shortly before the Whitsuntide break that my father sent me round to Mr Stephens' farm for help in mending the tractor. I had been using it in the field we call Bounds, which borders on to Stephens' farm, and the thing had packed up on me. My mother was out at Bakewell market, and Bounds was too far away for my father to get to, though if I could have brought the tractor down to the yard he could probably have seen to it; he was well enough for this now.

'Have I to fetch Alec Baxter?' I asked.

'You will not,' he said. He still wouldn't have a Baxter on his land, though Kathleen was one of them.

'Pop over to Bill Stephens,' he said. 'He'll not mind.'

Bill Stephens was at Bakewell too. I found his strange wife fussing over the hens in the back. I never liked her. Her teeth were brown, and her hair was loose and dusty. Her legs were heavily veined above the woollen ankle socks she always wore. Though her husband was nice enough, there was a trace of malice in her that I couldn't cope with; and a vagueness, as though while she was talking to you something far more important was occupying her mind. I watched her crooning over her hens now, ruffling their warm feathers as a child might, dangling her drab hair across their backs.

'We need some help with the tractor,' I explained.

She didn't look up. 'Don't tell me Madge Tanner's asking for help! Don't tell me Mrs High and Mighty is stooping this low!' she said to the hens.

'It's my father who sent me. But never mind – I'll manage.'

That was when Col Stephens came out of the barn. He must have been watching us.

'Wait, Jeannie. I'll come and have a look at it for you,' he said; and then to his mother, scolding her while she smiled wickedly at him: 'You knew I'd help, Mam. Why didn't you ask me?'

Col and I were in the same class once, but

he'd left two years ago. I'd hardly seen him since, though we were only fields away from each other. I'd not noticed how tall he'd grown, and how his voice had deepened properly now. I felt shy of him as we walked along towards Bounds together.

'Why did you dash off like that during Easter Ball?' he asked me. 'I wanted to dance with you, you know!'

'You never did,' I laughed, but uncomfortably. Why was he saying this to me?

'I did, too. Ask the lads. We all picked you out. But I was going to ask you first.'

'I had my father to see to,' I muttered. Wasn't he just saying it, to fill in the silence while we walked? Surely he'd just made it up out of his head? Or was it true – and if it was true, why did I find it so hard to return his smile, or to look at him at all for that matter, and why was my mouth as dry as paper? I was glad when we reached the tractor at last, and he settled down to the business of testing it. I watched him wonderingly.

'Will you show me what to do, so's I'll know next time?' I asked.

He laughed across at me, teasing. 'Little Miss

Independence! You're getting like your mam! Are you too good to ask a man for help?'

I nearly said 'And you're getting like your mother!' – and I would have done at one time, and walked off home, but I was more absorbed in the excitement his teasing eyes had caused in me, and which seemed to have taken control of me. Why him, when he'd never crossed my mind in years? Why now?

'D'you hear that old lark, Jeannie, watching us? And singing and singing as if all that great sky belonged to him, and he'll never run out of song to fill it with!'

'Perhaps we're the only ones listening to him,' I said. 'And he's singing just for us.'

Col Stephens met me that night at Bounds when I was doing the walk-around, and I was too late to meet Kathleen at the clough. I never even thought about her.

'Jeannie holds hands with Col Stephens by the bridge,' Marion said one night at tea. 'And paddles in the stream with him. I saw her.'

'That'll do!' said my mother, glancing quickly at me and away again, smiling.

'He's a nice lad, Colin,' my father said. 'Always was, like his dad. Straight.'

'But his mother's a right weirdo,' put in Marion.

'That'll *do*, Marion. Now!' My mother glanced at me again, and I felt her eyes on me even though I was staring out of the window, as though something very important was happening to the hens out in the yard. It was as though they were speaking of someone else, not me. I was alarmed and pleased at the same time that they had noticed about Col; and that they didn't mind.

He distracted me from my work all right, though I made a pretence of going up to my room every night to study. I could see the roofs of his farm buildings from my window, and wondered at the fact that I'd never noticed them before, and never sensed him moving about from room to room, helping his nice father, man to man at his work, and his strange mother watching jealously.

During my exam weeks he met me every day from school, and we'd walk or swim in the pool or lie in the long grass with the sun warm on us. At first I talked about the exams I'd just been doing, because I was so full of them, and he would say, 'You're too clever by far, Jeannie Tanner.' I hated him saying that. Acquired knowledge, that's all it was. Layer on layer of it, neatly pasted down like wallpaper. Was it to be like a race, or a creed, to divide us? If that was so, it wasn't worth having.

'Ah, Col Stephens, but you're the wise one!' I would say.

One day we took the bus to Castleton, and climbed Mam Tor. Nobody there but us, and all that sky, and all that lark-song.

'Let me keep this for ever!' I thought, and it seemed as if the happiness I felt was flowing into me through the air I was breathing, pulsing into my own blood-beat; and at the same time was draining away from me inexorably. We walked down into Winnat's Pass, deep in the hills' shadows, where the wind was cool.

'Listen to that wind, though,' I said. 'Doesn't it sound to you like a woman's voice, wailing?'

'It *is* a woman's voice,' he told me. 'They say two young lovers were murdered here, and that's her voice, crying out for anyone who can hear her.'

'And we're the only ones here!' I shivered with the chill the sound brought me.

'What will you do, Jeannie, now your exams are finished?' he asked me. University. He knew that. He knew it. I'd promised myself, and I'd promised my gran too, in a way. Mrs Kennedy in her Indian dress flashed in and out of my mind as though I'd put on a light and switched it off again.

'I don't have to go,' I said steadily. 'Maybe I won't pass my exams, anyway.'

He laughed. 'You'll pass, all right. You're too clever, that's your trouble. Too clever for the likes of me; and that's *our* trouble.'

We walked down to the little town in silence, but I blamed the wailing voice of Winnat's Pass for destroying that day for me.

One afternoon in the holidays I was waiting for Col near their farm. I saw his mother coming down the drive, and supposed she was off down to the village shop.

'Hello, Mrs Stephens!' I called, though my first reaction was to duck out of sight.

She didn't answer till she'd come right up to me. 'It's Jeannie this and Jeannie that, till I'm sick to death of hearing your name. Singing like a lovesick cow, and mooning round the house. It's pitiful!'

I smiled, sharing it with her, but she put her cold hands on my arms and pulled me towards her, shaking me. 'You're not having him, if that's what you're thinking. He's not wasting himself on the likes of you.'

She caught sight of Col coming towards us down the drive, and she scuttled off without another word. I never mentioned her to him, but I dreamt of her, witch-like, feeding him herbs to make him see me as she did: stuck-up, proud, scheming. But she was right about one thing. I did want him. I would have sacrificed anything, then, to be with him. I nearly did.

I prayed that I would fail my exams now. My hands were ice-cold the day the letter came with my results.

'Well?' my mother said. 'You're white as death, child. You've never failed?'

'I've passed,' I said, staring at the letter. 'But I've changed my mind. I'm not going.'

She shrugged, weary of me. 'It's your life.'

And my father: 'Just like a girl!', laughing.

They didn't care. What did they know about sacrifice?

Mrs Kennedy rang me, and I told her the same thing. It seemed years since I'd seen her. I told myself I hated the way she dressed; her earnestness. How could I have wanted to be like her?

'I think it's a waste, Jeannie, don't you? But if it's your choice . . .'

I put the receiver down while she was still talking. I felt sick with shame. But my sacrifice was for Col. I'd never wanted to give so much to one person before; perhaps I never would again. He would have done the same for me, I told myself.

That night I ran to Bounds to meet him. 'Guess what!' I laughed. 'It's all right! I failed!'

It was easy saying it. Easy. I thought of his mother, scratching for eggs among the hens, thinking herself rid of me, and I felt jubilant. I was proud of myself for not listening to her, or to Mrs Kennedy. I'd made my own choice. But Col was silent for a long time.

'You are pleased, aren't you?'

'I wanted to surprise you,' he said at last. 'I'd been saving it for today to tell you. I've got myself into the agricultural college at Oxford. We'd have been there together.'

Joy surged up again, and at the same time drained away, like the last light of evening. 'You won't still go, though?' I prompted him. 'Not without me?' My perverseness dragged me towards this last hurdle. I could hear the lark now all right, separating us with its brutal song in our sad silence.

I took my university place, and he came to his college. We do see each other from time to time, both strangers in this town, too busy to stop and talk. Funny, how close we were, and how distant now. Strange, too, how hurt I always feel when I think of him and of what I learnt from him. I'll never forget those last few words we said to each other by the old stone wall that told us which land was ours; which theirs.

'You won't still go, without me?' I said.

'Of course I'll go. You wouldn't want me to do anything else, would you? I've got my own future to think of now, Jeannie. And you've got yours.'

Reunion

When I came home again for my first holiday that Christmas, the train rushed me back into the valley before I had time to prepare myself for its loveliness. The hills seemed to open their arms to welcome me. Why should they fill me with such sadness?

Marion had come to the station to meet me, and her excited dancing on the platform drove my strange melancholy away.

'Jeannie! It's going to be a fantastic Christmas!' she shouted, before I was off the train even. 'Guess what? I'm getting a piano! And guess what . . . Dad can walk down the lane and back all on his own. And guess what . . . !'

'What?' I laughed, scooping her in my arms. 'Martin's back.'

I hadn't seen Martin for over two years. He'd filled out a lot, and was bearded. His clothes had style, even though they were casual, and he was full of himself. He showed us his folder of paintings. I felt shy of him, and of the rush of warmth I felt when I saw him and my father joking and laughing together. He put a new painting of the farmhouse over the mantelpiece.

'I don't know what to make of you three,' my father said grudgingly. 'Martin and his paintings . . . and all Marion can think of is music . . . I've had to tout round for an old piano for her. Piano! And Lord knows what you've got in your head, Jeannie. I don't know where you all get it from, but it's not from me, that's for sure.'

My mother smiled proudly.

'And I've never seen much of it in you either, so you needn't look so smug,' he added.

'Depends whether you come from farming stock or thinking stock,' she said. 'My mother had a brain or two in her head, remember.'

'It's nothing to do with brains,' Martin put in. 'It's a different way of looking at things. We all have to look at things in our own way.'

'I suppose we have, Martin,' said my father quietly.

He's changed, I thought. Even in those few months I'd been away it seemed to me that he was different. He and my mother seemed to be different towards each other; even in this bantering talk they were not at odds. Now she said to him, 'The mistake you made was to turn away the only one of the four who was of real farming stock. You misjudged our Kathleen, all right.'

Dangerous ground; but still my father smiled. 'She's proved herself, that one. She's the finest sort of woman any farmer could want for a wife. Like you, Madge.'

My mother glanced at me, and blushed like a girl. Martin winked at me from behind her.

'Ask him now!' Marion whispered. Mum shook her head, but my father asked sharply: 'Ask him what?'

'Nothing,' Mum said. 'Later.'

'Ask him what?' my father repeated, grasping Marion's hand, only half in play.

'If Kathleen can come home for Christmas dinner.' Tears had blurted into Marion's eyes, but she spoke up bravely. 'It's not fair; if Martin and Jeannie are here for Christmas, Kathleen should be home, too.'

My mother sighed, and went back to her preparation of the meal. 'She has her own home,' she said quietly.

But Marion persisted. 'Can't we just *ask* her? Dad?'

He leaned forward stiffly from his straight chair and prodded the logs in the fire. 'We can ask her,' he said. 'I doubt she'll come.'

'And Alec.'

It seemed that the tension that had built up so rapidly in my father was just as rapidly released. He glanced quickly across at my mother. 'All right. Alec too,' he said.

Nothing would do for Marion now but that she and I should go over the fields straightaway with Kathleen's invitation. My wellingtons stood where they had always done, in the porch, and my old duffle was hanging behind the door.

Marion half ran in her excitement, singing Christmas carols into the cold air as she went.

'You've a pretty little voice, Marion,' I said, and realized it was the only time I'd told her that. She seemed a real person now, not just a scurrying secretive little thing to be played with and scolded. Was it just because I'd been away that everyone seemed different? Or was I the one who'd changed?

She preened back her lovely bright hair. 'I know,' she said. 'I'm going to be a pop star, I should think. I was the angel Gabriel in the school play. I'm getting a piano, Jeannie . . .'

'Yes,' I laughed. 'You told me.'

'Isn't it going to be a lovely Christmas!' She danced across the frosted stubble, arms flung wide. 'Everything's going right. It's because Dad's better.'

Over the next few days I began to pick up the pieces of the months that I'd missed. The farm began to lose its strangeness, and I was back into the familiar way of chatting to my mother at the kitchen table as we prepared vegetables together. She told me that she'd been taking my father up into the fields as far as she could get in the Land Rover, and that together they'd worked slowly, piece by piece, at the wall-mending and winter chores that had to be done. Marion had done her share of the cooking, and in the evenings my father had come back exhausted, hungry, and thoroughly satisfied with himself. They did the books together, and twice now he'd been down to Hope market with her.

'And guess who we saw there?' Marion interrupted her. 'Will o'by Twist!'

'Poor Wilby Hodge,' Mum sighed. 'But he's done all right for himself, Jeannie. He works for a farmer in Baslow. He's got his own cottage now too. He's all right.'

'Did my father see him?' I asked, remembering the terrible day of my father's return from hospital to find Wilby in his working jacket.

'He did,' said my mother. 'And they had more than a few drinks together at the Cheese. He's a brave man, your father,' she added suddenly.

'He's had to fight his pride a few times over the last few years. It's not been easy for him.'

'It's been a lot worse for you.'

Marion had slipped off her stool and wandered out into the yard. Mum watched her go before she said simply: 'Yes. It has. I could have left him at one time, Jeannie. Imagine that! I nearly left him.'

I turned away, ashamed of my embarrassment and of the guilty memory of my plan for her to move out into Aunt Jessie's. What would that have done for my father? Would he be walking again now? I could just see him through the window, walking from the sheds with Martin, leaning as he was against his shoulder, and laughing as they crossed the slippery slope to the muck pit. Would he have had logs piled up ready for the evening, and winter flowers on the windowsill?

'Is everything all right now?' I asked awkwardly.

'More than all right. I think we understand each other now. I must love the man, I suppose!' she laughed.

I wish I was like Kathleen. She'd have hugged

Mum at that, and probably danced her round the kitchen.

But Kathleen didn't dance on Christmas Day. She came in quietly with Alec, and the two of them sat in silence while my mother and Aunt Jessie and I put the last preparations to the meal.

'You all right, Kathleen?' my mother asked.

'Of course.'

'Well, you don't look it.'

'Long face on her,' my father retorted, disappointed.

When the meal was served she ate a little, and then excused herself and went outside. We said nothing. Alec looked embarrassed. After a while she came back, looking very white and strained, and sat down again. She messed about with her food, not eating. My father couldn't contain himself.

'You didn't have to come,' he reminded her. 'But seeing as you have, get it down you. It's the biggest bird we've had, and I killed it myself.'

'I can't,' said Kathleen weakly. 'I've just been sick.'

'She's pregnant, you know,' said Marion earnestly. 'I could tell as soon as I saw her.'

In the laughter and congratulations that followed Martin slipped down to the cellar for more wine, and we toasted the good news, even though poor old Kathleen could only manage water. The colour had come back to her cheeks when she saw how pleased everyone was. My father shook Alec's hand warmly.

'If there's one thing your father can't resist, it's babies,' my mother said, and he laughed.

'That's right, lambs and babies, they're all the same to me. Magic.'

'It's nothing to be miserable about, Kathleen,' Aunt Jessie said. 'Good heavens, I'd thought you'd lost all your money.'

'That's the trouble,' Kathleen said, glancing at Alec. 'We haven't got any.'

Alec frowned at her.

'Your mother must be pleased, Alec,' Mum said. 'First grandchild.'

'I suppose so, Mrs Tanner,' he said. 'But it's going to be a squeeze, with a baby. Our Tony's getting married . . . They'll live in, too. And our

Pete's just left school. He's at home all day. Five men in the house, and we all want to farm. My dad hasn't got enough jobs for us all.'

'You couldn't do anything else but sheep-farming, I suppose?' my father asked him.

'I wouldn't!' Alec said.

The year before Alec met Kathleen he'd worked his way round the world as a sheepman, shearing. He'd started off in the south of England, where they shear early, in April, and he'd worked his way north, to Scotland, across to Norway, down to South Africa, and over to New Zealand. 'I could earn £120 a day, then,' he told us. 'And I loved every second of it. I could live with sheep, quite easily.'

I knew what it was like to shear a sheep. It was like wrestling with a two hundredweight sack of live potatoes, till your back could break with the pain of it.

'Anyway,' Alec finished up. 'I can't do that again. Not now.'

He touched Kathleen's hand, but she drew it back. 'I don't know about you living with the sheep. We might all have to, baby and all!'

'We'll manage,' he coaxed her. 'We've applied to manage a National Trust farm. But we're going to stay in Derbyshire, and we're going to stick with sheep-farming. We'll just have to wait.'

There was a long silence in the room. We listened to the logs crackling, and the rowan scratching at the window. The kittens pawed at the chairs, and, unnoticed, Marion dropped them turkey scraps.

Then my father leaned across to Martin and tapped his arm. 'What about it, eh? What do you think? Is it theirs for the taking?'

Only Martin knew what he was talking about. 'Don't ask me that, Dad,' he said.

'What do you mean, John?' my mother asked. 'Is what theirs for the taking?'

He waved his arm vaguely. 'This. The farm.' Nobody spoke.

'I've a son who doesn't want it, and a son-in-law who needs it. That's all.'

Martin jerked himself stubbornly back from the table.

'Don't, Dad,' said Kathleen. 'We weren't saying that.'

'I know,' he acknowledged. 'But I am. It's to be faced. It's time this lad made up his mind, what he does want.'

Martin was standing by the window now, his hands thrust deep in his pockets, staring out at the winter-dark hills.

'I do want the farm,' he said at last. 'But not yet. I haven't finished my course yet. I haven't travelled. I haven't done any real painting. If I come back before I'm ready, I'll never settle. I don't suppose that satisfies you, though.'

But this was exactly the answer my father wanted. White Peak Farm was Martin's to inherit: always was; always will be. My father wouldn't have wanted it any other way.

'Well then, there's a home and job here till you get your own farm to run,' he told Alec. 'If you want it. You can have Martin's room. Plenty of room in there for a cot or two. It's high time we had another baby in the house. I don't know where this big girl's come from.'

He winked at Marion. I remembered how he used to coddle and fondle Marion when she was a tiny baby, and how jealous I'd always been of her then. But that was him; tender one minute, and in a passion of anger the next. A baby himself, sometimes.

'Good,' said my mother, pouring out more wine. 'We'll celebrate, then, shall we?' But she spoke in a tight, tired voice, and she didn't look at my father once.

It was later, when we were doing the washing-up together, that Aunt Jessie came up with a much better idea. She thought my father was mistaken in inviting Alec and Kathleen to live at the farm.

'Madge and John are better off without other people in the house,' she said. 'Your mother's worked that hard to put things right between them, though I don't expect you to understand what I'm talking about, Jeannie. They're only just finding out how to get on with each other, after all these years, that's what it is. For goodness' sake . . . another married couple in the house! That's all they need! That'll put an end to *their* lovey-doving!'

I didn't dare ask whose.

'And anyway,' Aunt Jessie went on, 'Alec

Baxter's an experienced sheepman. If he's to help your father out, and Lord knows he'll need help if he's to build his stock up again the way he wants to, then he should be getting a proper wage for it, not board. Specially now he's looking out for his own farm.'

By the time she'd worked through the great mound of dishes she was drying, Aunt Jessie had talked herself into offering Alec and Kathleen her upstairs room as a flat, provided they didn't move her fox.

Then the celebrating began, all right. I watched them all, dancing all in their own way to my father's old records, and I felt again the odd pang I'd felt when I was coming back home to the valley and I saw the forgotten hills.

What was it?

The celebrating continued till after midnight. Alec and Kathleen took Aunt Jessie back to the cottage that was soon to be their home, too. Marion had sung herself to sleep upstairs. Martin was sketching at the table, and my father, old suddenly, was asleep in his chair by the fire. I went out into the yard with my mother to check the sheds, and to say goodnight to the cockerel on his post. I had forgotten how black the sky could be out here, and how brilliant the stars. I had forgotten how the night air sharpened the sweet smell of the milking sheds.

I listened to the sheep coughing in far fields, and to the rush of cold streams seeping from our hill down to the river. An owl hooted from his tree in the dark lane.

'Jeannie? Coming in?'

'In a minute, Mum.'

'What do you think you'll be doing when your course finishes?' she asked me, sensing my mood. 'Back home?'

I couldn't answer her. In spite of everything, I knew that my wings were bent for flying. Gran would have understood. So far to go. So many things to do.

My mother said, 'I think you'll be the one to leave. Don't worry, girl . . . no matter what you do with your life you'll always make your way back to White Peak Farm.'

* * *

Yes.

I always will.

PRAISE FOR BERLIE DOHERTY

'Berlie Doherty captures the magic of human emotion'
Grace Kempster, *Books for Keeps*

'Some children's authors show off by making their
writing all high-blown swords-and-sorcery and some go
the other way and make it all too simple. But Berlie
pitches it just right. She has a fantastic prose style, plus a
great feel for characters and situations'
Ian McMillan

'Berlie Doherty writes both for adults and children,
moving easily across the divide'
Guardian

'What a marvellous writer . . . one who uses language
as if it has been newly invented'
Junior Bookshelf

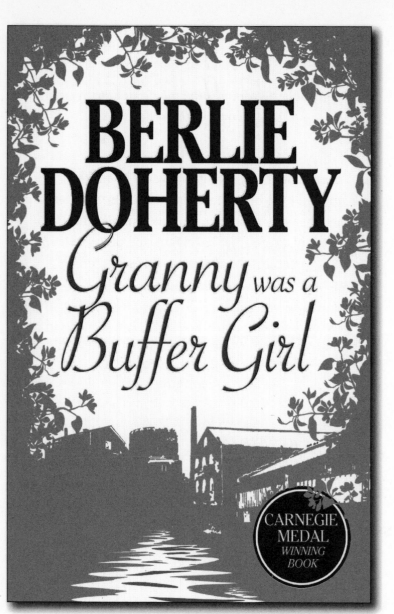

BERLIE DOHERTY

Granny was a Buffer Girl

Granny was a Buffer Girl

by Berlie Doherty

'You tell your secrets, and I'll tell mine,'
said Granny Dorothy. 'I'll tell you something that Albert
doesn't know, even. My best secret.'

Mum did catch my eye then, and her look promised me
that I wouldn't be going away from home without sharing
all its secrets, and all its love stories, and all its ghost
stories too.

Jess is 18 and leaving home for the first time.
Her family get together to celebrate and share their stories
of their lives – stories of love and adventure, of happiness
and loss, of promises and secrets.

"A compelling and unusual book" TIMES EDUCATIONAL SUPPLEMENT

"Vividly evocative of time and place, a poignant portrait of a dozen
individuals whose joys and trials are universal" KIRKUS

WINNER OF THE CARNEGIE MEDAL

An amazing adventure
begins in the big house
by the Mersey

BERLIE DOHERTY

The Sailing Ship Tree

The Sailing Ship Tree
A Liverpool Story

by Berlie Doherty

This is the story of the Big House by the Mersey and the people who lived there. In particular the twins Walter and Dorothy, whose father is the butler; Master George, the desperately lonely son of the wealthy owner; and Tweeny, the little maid treated hardly better than a slave.

In a way the house belongs to all of them, though the lives of the servants and masters couldn't be more different.

When disaster strikes, and Master George needs help, the four children find refuge in the branches of a beautiful chestnut tree in the grounds of the house and there create a daring plot to help him escape to a new world.

"Another triumph from Berlie Doherty" SUNDAY TELEGRAPH

"This beautifully crafted, elegiac novel operates equally successfully on two levels – as a work of fiction and a social document"
BOOKS FOR KEEPS

Berlie Doherty

Winner of the Carnegie Medal

Children of Winter

Will the plague destroy them all?

CHILDREN OF WINTER

by Berlie Doherty

Out walking, deep in the Derbyshire hills, Catherine and her family are forced to take shelter from a sudden storm in an old barn.

It all seems strangely familiar to Catherine. As the torchlight dims, shadows of the past crowd in, memories of a time hundreds of years ago, when three children took refuge in a barn, not from a storm, but from a terrible plague ...

This gripping and haunting adventure is inspired by the true story of the village of Eyam which in 1665 cut itself off from the rest of Derbyshire, so that no other village would catch the Plague.

"Vividly and sensitively realised" GUARDIAN

THE FILE ON

Fraulein Berg

It's hard to spot the enemy within

Joan Lingard

The File on Fraulein Berg

by Joan Lingard

1944. Belfast. The War drags on. Kate, Harriet and Sally read spy stories and imagine themselves dropping over enemy lines to perform deeds of great daring.

When Fraulein Berg, a real German, arrives at their school it doesn't take them long to work out that their new teacher is a spy. Now the girls have a mission. To watch her. Follow her. Track down her every secret.
Prove she is the enemy.

But the File on Fraulein Berg reveals a very different story – one that will haunt Kate for the rest of her life.

A classic story from the award-winning author of the Kevin and Sadie *books*